William Latham Bevan

The Case of the Church in Wales

William Latham Bevan

The Case of the Church in Wales

ISBN/EAN: 9783337329754

Printed in Europe, USA, Canada, Australia, Japan

Cover: Foto ©Andreas Hilbeck / pixelio.de

More available books at **www.hansebooks.com**

THE
CASE OF THE CHURCH IN WALES.

AN ESSAY

BY THE

REV. W. L. BEVAN, M.A.,

CANON OF ST. DAVID'S, AND VICAR OF HAY,

AUTHOR OF "LETTERS TO LIBERATIONISTS."
"REPLY TO MR. H. RICHARD," "TWO ESSAYS ON THE CHURCH IN WALES."

PRICE SIXPENCE.

London:

THE CHURCH DEFENCE INSTITUTION,
9, BRIDGE STREET, WESTMINSTER, S.W.

PREFACE.

IN the following Essay the Author has endeavoured to present in a concise and connected form the substance of former Essays, composed, as occasion arose, on separate topics connected with the past history and present position of the Church in Wales. He has found the task more difficult, and the result less satisfactory, than he had anticipated. Dealing, as he has proposed, mainly with charges of inefficiency brought against the Church by Liberationists, it may very possibly seem to the friends of the Church that he has given such prominence to this topic as to shut out of view the many favourable signs of revived energy and success which greet the eye in almost every part of Wales. But unless the Essay had been extended to greater length, it was absolutely impossible to deal satisfactorily with every aspect of the subject, and the Author must beg his readers to bear in mind the limited scope of his enquiry, which is to expose the fallacies and exaggerations of Liberationist orators in their attempts to depreciate the Church in the eyes of the public. To a certain extent he feels himself relieved of the duty of vindicating the present character of the Church by the admissions of her assailants, who, for the most part, are ready to acknowledge the marked revival of life and energy in her midst, though they qualify such admissions with the assertion that nothing comes of it all. We may accept their admission, and leave it to time and observation to show whether life and energy will prove to be fruitless.

March 1st, 1886.

THE CASE

OF

THE CHURCH IN WALES.

CHAPTER I.

SECT. 1.—The object which the author of this Essay has in
view is not to deny, or even extenuate the shortcomings of the
Church in Wales, but to define (as far as may be) their true
extent and character, and to refer them to their true causes.
He does not address himself to Liberationists : he is willing
at the outset to concede to them all that they seem to
think requisite to justify their measures against the Church,
namely, that it is in a minority as compared with Nonconformity. His admission of the fact must not be regarded as
an admission of the justice of the claim which Liberationists
have founded upon it. But a discussion on this point would
lead him away from his present object, which is concerned
rather with the credit, than with the property or position of
the Church. It is in the hope that there exists outside the
circle of Liberationism a body of judicially minded persons,
both among Welsh Nonconformists and English Churchmen,

B

who are willing to sift the truth of the charges brought
against the Church in Wales, and to take other matters into
consideration beyond the mere fact of its being in a
minority, that the author ventures to put forth the following
plea.

SECT. 2.—The charges alleged against the Church in
Wales may be summarised under the following three heads :
that it is an alien institution; that it has been negligent
and corrupt; and that it is now a failure. We place these
charges in the sequence which they hold in the argument
of its assailants, their contention (as we understand it)
being that the specific cause of the failure and other defects
attributed to the Church in Wales, is its alien character.
As we do not recognise the truth of the sequence, we shall
give precedence to the accusation of failure, with a view to
show that the degree to which it exists has been grossly
exaggerated, and that the *weakness* (rather than "failure")
which we acknowledge to exist is attributable to other
causes than those above mentioned.

SECT. 3.—The charge of failure has been formulated by
Mr. Llewellyn Dillwyn, M.P. for Swansea Town, in the
following terms, extracted from his Parliamentary motion
on the Disestablishment of the Church in Wales :—"That
it has failed in its professed object of promoting the
interests of the Welsh people, and ministers only to a small
minority." We have here two distinct allegations ; one that
the Church has failed to promote the interests of the Welsh
people, the other that it ministers only to a small minority.
These, we say, are distinct allegations, which may be
separately discussed and which are not necessarily con-
sequent one upon the other. It is clearly possible that the
Church may, according to its means and opportunities, have
promoted the interests of the Welsh people, and yet have
failed to secure a majority of adherents. But no attention,
as far as we know, has been paid to the distinctness of these

allegations, it being assumed that no further evidence of the truth of the first is needed than what is supplied by the second. The effect of this has been to narrow the field of observation, shutting out a great deal that might be said as to various ways in which the Church has promoted the interests of the Welsh people, and basing the whole case against it on the mere question of which is at the present moment the strongest—the Church or Nonconformity. We protest against such a restriction, and we request our readers to bear in mind the distinctness of these propositions, while we proceed to follow Mr. Dillwyn in his allegation as to the Church ministering only to a small minority.

SECT. 4.—Mr. Dillwyn's evidence that the Church ministers only to a small minority was laid before the public in a speech which he delivered at the time of the Liberationist Conference, at Swansea, in 1884. Before detailing that evidence, it may prove serviceable to English readers if we point out an ambiguity attaching to the terms "Wales" and "Welsh," which has led to a considerable amount of confusion. Wales proper consists (as everyone knows) of the twelve counties specified in the Act of Henry VIII.; but in addition to this, the name is popularly used as inclusive of Monmouthshire, which belongs, both ethnographically and geographically, to the same district. These two are included in a single Registration division, as given in the Census Report, but with different areas and populations from those which belong to the counties proper.* The

---

* The variety of areas to which we have above adverted originates in the fact that Wales has no natural boundary on the side of England, in other words, is not a separate country from England. The boundary is a purely artificial one, and is frequently unmarked even by a brook. The valleys of the Severn, Wye and Dee open out towards England, and the routes lie open along the northern and southern coasts. The absence of all natural boundary has a bearing on the

expression "Welsh" similarly applies to various areas according as the topic under discussion may require. The "Welsh Church," for instance, might either be used for the four Welsh dioceses, which include parts of England (viz., Monmouthshire and a portion of Shropshire), but do not include the whole of Wales, inasmuch as portions of Radnorshire and Montgomeryshire belong to the diocese of Hereford; or again, it may be used as descriptive of that which is distinctive of the Church in Wales, namely, its language, its history and traditions: and so, again, the expression "Welsh people" may be used to designate exclusively the Welsh-speaking people as distinct from the other inhabitants of Wales. Lastly, we may notice that Welsh Nonconformity has been introduced into the large towns of England where colonies of Welshmen have settled, and that in some cases the congregations are included in the reports of the Nonconformist bodies. It is important to keep these distinctions in view, particularly in connection with Nonconformist statistics. Neither in his motion nor in his statistical statement has Mr. Dillwyn recognised the distinctions marked out in the foregoing sentences. By using the expression "Welsh people" without any explanation, he conveys to the public mind a very exaggerated idea of the shortcomings of the Church. Unless we are much mistaken, nine out of ten Englishmen would understand by "Welsh people" the population of Wales as a whole. But what is Mr. Dillwyn's own explanation as reported in the *South Wales Daily News?* "No doubt the Church promoted the interests of its own communion. But he would ask any one who knew Wales whether, if the rich people left Wales proper, from

general question of special legislation for Wales. Those who live in proximity to the border feel it to be an anomaly that two parishes in all respects of similar character, and maintaining constant intercourse with each other, should be placed under different laws.

which he excluded the large towns where there was a considerable population of English, they believed there would be
any Church at all in Wales." These are very large deductions
from the population of Wales: and if (as we assume) Mr.
Dillwyn would extend his remarks to the English-speaking
areas in the border counties and in South Pembrokeshire;
and if we add to these a large number of Welsh-speaking
people who receive the ministrations of the Church, it is
difficult to say what would be the numerical value of the
population which he exempts from his accusation. But of
all this there is no inkling whatever in the terms of his
motion. Then as to his statistical statement, which was
drawn up in a way peculiar to Liberationists by making the
number of Churchmen to depend on the number of Nonconformists, the former being represented by the balance
left after deducting the latter (together with the non-
worshippers) from the gross population, we find most serious
deductions made from the number of Churchmen by trans-
ferring to Wales proper figures that belong to other areas.
Instead of taking the population of Wales proper he has
taken that of Wales as a Registration division and has thus
reduced Churchmen by 16,000; though professing to quote
Nonconformist returns applying to Wales alone, he has
included 10,570 Calvinistic Methodists in Monmouthshire,
40 congregations of the same body living in the border
counties, 7,579 Congregationalists living in various parts of
England, and about 25,000 Wesleyans living outside of
Wales—these numbers being in each case exclusive of
children—and the correction of these errors alone would go
far to raise the number of Churchmen some 50 per cent.*

---

* Mr. Dillwyn's statement was as follows :—"The Congregationalists
number 253,016; the Calvinistic Methodists, 250,274; Baptists,
144,307; Wesleyans, 78,580; Primitive Methodists, 17,767; other
sects, 8,000; making a total of 751,944. The population of Wales
in 1881 was 1,343,227. Deducting the Nonconformists as above,

The same errors (with the exception of the 10,570 Calvinistic Methodists) were made by Dr. Rees in estimating the number of Churchmen for Wales and Monmouthshire ; and he made a further addition to the Nonconformist side of no less than 24,861 Calvinistic Methodists living in other parts of England, and about 27,000 Baptists to bring them up to the round number of 200,000.* The statements of Mr. Dillwyn and Dr. Rees, though delivered on the same occa-

---

268,645 children under four years of age, taken as one-fifth of the population, and, say, 30,000 Roman Catholics and 150,000 of no religion, that left to be accounted for, as belonging to the Church, 142,639." It will be observed that on this method of calculation every error in the preceding items affects the number of Churchmen. We have already specified erroneous additions to the Nonconformists amounting to about 50,000 (allowing 8,000 for the 40 congregations), and we have yet to reduce by a large amount the number of children, so that Mr. Dillwyn should have stated the balance of Churchmen at something like 330,000 without or 370,000 with children.

 * Dr. Rees's computation resembles Mr. Dillwyn's in its structure, but differs from it both as respects area (Monmouthshire being included by the former), and also as respects the errors introduced into it. It runs as follows :—" Congregationalists, 276,201 ; Calvinistic Methodists, 274,603 ; Baptists, 200,000; Wesleyans, 86,438; Primitive Methodists, 19,382; other sects, 10,000 ; making a total of 866,626 Nonconformist members and hearers. Add children under five above 200,000, and this brings the Nonconformist numbers to 1,100,000, leaving a balance of 474,000 from the population. From this subtract 30,000 Roman Catholics, and non-religious 224,000. There will be left 220,000 for Churchmen." It is but fair to state that Sir Hussey Vivian, M.P., denies that Dr. Rees committed any error of the kind imputed to him. In a correspondence which took place in the *Western Mail* between himself and the author of this Essay, and which has since been published in pamphlet form, under the title of " Welsh Denominational Statistics," he allows that Dr. Rees included 7,579 Congregationalists and 24,861 Calvinistic Methodists, who were living outside the specified area of the 13 counties, but he somehow finds in this fact evidence that Dr. Rees did not include Welshmen living in England. His words are these :—" In the above-named work (viz., Dr. Rees's " History of Nonconformity ") he gives 32,440 as belonging to the Congregationalist and Calvinistic Methodist denominations alone. It is, therefore, abundantly evident that in claiming 1,100,000 as the Non-

sion, apply (be it observed) to different areas, and it would appear as though Liberationist leaders had not agreed among themselves as to what is to be included under the Dis-establishment of the Church in Wales—whether it is to be confined to Wales proper (including the parishes now in an English diocese), or whether it is to be extended so as to take in parts of England itself. The errors already noticed conduced, of course, to make the Church a "small" minority. as expressed in the terms of Mr. Dillwyn's motion. There are, however, in these calculations other elements which con-tribute to the same result. We refer to the items of the non-worshippers, or irreligious section, and the children. As to the former, their number is a pure matter of conjecture; consequently the statistician has it in his power to enlarge or diminish it as suits his purpose. Dr. Rees estimated it in his "History of Nonconformity" at "half a million of men and women," exclusive (as we suppose) of children; but, finding that by so large an estimate he had crowded out the whole body of Churchmen, he felt no difficulty in reducing the number, without a word of explanation. to 224,000. inclusive of children, while Mr. Dillwyn kept him in coun-tenance by placing the number at 150,000 for the 12 counties, exclusive of children. But what value can possibly attach to statistical statements which admit of such varia-tions as exist between Dr. Rees in his "History" and Dr. Rees in his speech, though the interval between them was one of only a few months? Anything may be proved by such a method. A similar latitude was taken in reference to the children: Mr. Dillwyn placed his limit at four years of age and Dr. Rees at five years, while Sir Hussey Vivian

See Appen-dix A, p. 78.

p. 165.

conformist numbers for Wales and Monmouthshire, Dr. Rees did not include Welshmen living in England." We confess our inability to grasp this argument: the 32,440 were undoubtedly included in the 1,100,000, and therefore supply evidence that residents in England were included.

(as quoted in the Report on Intermediate Education in Wales), in a speech delivered in the House of Commons on the educational question, advanced it to 10 years. However, it made little difference what age was *stated*, inasmuch as the proportion assumed to exist between the children and the population did not perceptibly differ in the three cases. Yet it seems singular that the number of children under four should be equal, or nearly so, to the number under 10. We do not, of course, pretend to know where the limit lies at which Nonconformists regard a child as a "hearer." It probably is a varying one, according to the judgment of individuals. But why should the number of Churchmen be made to depend on such an element of uncertainty as this? And why should not statisticians who choose to state a certain age make their calculations according to that age, instead of putting down at random such a number of children as suits their purpose? Both Mr. Dillwyn and Dr. Rees exaggerated the number enormously, enhancing thereby the strength of Nonconformity and diminishing to an equal extent the strength of the Church. The impression which the examination of these statistical statements conveys to the mind is (to speak plainly) this—that the conclusion had been fixed before the calculation was entered upon. Dr. Rees had decided that Churchmen were not to be more than one-seventh of the population; and the items of the account were adjusted to make them appear as such. The same conclusion was intended doubtless to be arrived at by Mr. Dillwyn, but by inadvertence he estimated it at one-ninth instead of one-seventh, not having observed apparently that his balance of Churchmen was exclusive of children. The only result that can in any way be extracted from these statements is that the Nonconformists claim about five-ninths of the population. As to the remaining four-ninths they tell in reality nothing. We neither accept nor reject that estimate; we merely state the effect of the figures laid before us.

Sect. 5.—Thus far we have treated the denominational statistics of Wales as a whole : we have shown that the number of Nonconformists has been exaggerated by unwarrantable additions of various kinds with a view to crowd out Churchmen, and that when these additions are removed and the statements of Mr. Dillwyn and Dr. Rees are rectified, the proportions between Church and Nonconformity will be largely altered. It will tend to confirm this conclusion and to elucidate the general question if we look a little closer into these denominational statistics, and observe them by counties, or groups of counties. We may, for instance, compare the border counties with the interior counties. It will be found (if we mistake not) that the great strength of Nonconformity lies in the second of these divisions. Taking the statistics of the four chief bodies, Congregationalists, Calvinistic Methodists, Baptists, and Wesleyans —as given in Dr. Rees's " History," for the two first, in the "Handbook" and "Minutes of Conference" for the two last, we come to the conclusion that while the seven border counties (Monmouth and Glamorgan included) contain two-thirds of the population, they cannot claim much more than half the number of Nonconformists : consequently the remaining half is all concentrated in the one-third of the population which occupies the six interior or western counties. A further conclusion flowing out of this subdivision is this : that in the seven border counties there is a much larger residuum of population outside the pale of Nonconformity than Dr. Rees allows for the whole of Wales—a circumstance which tends to show the fallaciousness of his whole calculation. It is, therefore, quite impossible to say (except in the language of pure hyperbole) of two-thirds of Wales that the inhabitants are a "nation of Nonconformists"; a moiety of that section of the population are not Nonconformists, whatever else they may be, and there is abundance of room left for strength and vigour in the Church. This important

feature, however, is disguised by the abnormal returns of the
Nonconformists in the other six counties. If the correctness
of those returns can be sustained, then it must be allowed
that in that part of the country the inhabitants are a nation
of Nonconformists; under any circumstances it must be
conceded that Nonconformity is largely predominant there—
pre-eminently so in the Counties of Merioneth, Carnarvon
and Anglesea, and in a less degree in the three counties of
South Wales, where the Church is strong in various districts.
But whether the Nonconformist returns can be sustained, is
a question on which each person must form his own
judgment: and in order to supply some materials for such
a purpose, we will state the ratios which the "members,"
that is, *communicants*, of the four leading denominations
jointly, bear to the population of each county. They are as
follow:—Pembroke 26 per cent., Anglesea 31 per cent.,
Carmarthen 34 per cent., Carnarvon 32 per cent., Cardigan
39 per cent., and Merioneth 34 per cent. Now, let anyone
consider what is meant by a percentage, say, of 33 per cent.
of communicants to the population. Deducting 37 per
cent. from the total population for children under the age
of membership (say 15), there would remain 30 per
cent. for non-communicants of those bodies and all other
persons over the age of 15. This, it may be said, is not
impossible: a population may be so well worked up, that
the non-communicants may be reduced to a *minimum*
or even to *nil;* and Nonconformist leaders may claim that
they have achieved this in parts of Wales, though in point
of fact, they acknowledge an appreciable number of hearers
as distinct from members. But what is the case before
us? Not only 33 per cent., but 34 per cent. and even
up to 39 per cent. are claimed by four bodies alone, to the
exclusion of the minor bodies of Nonconformists, the
Church, Roman Catholics, and the non-religious section.
Without saying that this is impossible, is it probable? It

is absurd to say that there are absolutely no Churchmen in those counties: they are found in considerable force in the neighbourhoods of Carnarvon and Bangor, and along the coast line eastward of the latter place; they hold no unimportant place in Cardiganshire, from which they are practically excluded by the Nonconformist statistics; and though in the country parishes of other counties (South Pembrokeshire excluded, where they are present in force) they may be but thinly strewn, yet the aggregate number of these would tell in a percentage. Room must be found for such Churchmen as exist, and we question whether the denominational returns allow of any. Is their existence, then, to be ignored on the evidence of returns which are not open to our inspection? And are these returns to affect the Church, not only in the localities to which they apply, but throughout the whole of Wales? We have still to draw the attention of the reader to the fact that, if these returns are correct, there can be no irreligious people in some counties of North Wales. But can this be true? We fancy that we have heard of their existence from Nonconformist sources of information: but the returns leave no room for them. However, not to discuss these details, we may assert that the point to which we have adverted is one of the greatest importance for a sound judgment on the religious condition of Wales. The proportion of Nonconformists in the six counties containing one-third of the population is double of that in the seven counties containing two-thirds of the population. If the sufficiency of Nonconformity for the wants and aspirations of the people is to form the ground of the Church's condemnation, the area to which any legislation founded on that condition should extend, ought in justice to be restricted to those districts within which Nonconformity has met with such marked, though possibly exaggerated, success.

CHAPTER II.

Sect. 1.—We may at this point deviate somewhat from
our immediate purpose to notice the linguistic condition of
Wales, which has formed an important factor in settling the
relative positions of Church and Dissent. The leading
authority on this subject is Mr. Ravenstein, who read a
paper on it before the Statistical Society, which is published
in its journal for 1879. Whether there are *data* sufficient
for dealing with so variable an element as bi-lingualism
we will not undertake to say. Suffice it that Mr. Ravenstein has done all that could be done. Some misapprehen-
sion has gone abroad as to the result of his inquiries. The
Report of the Departmental Committee on Intermediate
Education quotes it thus:—"Out of a population of 1,426,514
in Wales and Monmouthshire no less than 1.006,100 habitually speak Welsh." We deem this neither a correct nor a
complete version of Mr. Ravenstein's opinion. The number
stated includes the Welsh-speaking population living outside the specified area, and the word " habitually " is an
interpolation. The number of Welsh-speaking people in
Wales was given as 934,530, and of these Mr. Ravenstein
estimated that 640,420 spoke both Welsh and English ; in

what proportions théy used either language he did not attempt to define, and it is therefore incorrect to say that àll bi-lingualists *habitually* speak Welsh. The mere fact that they *can* speak English implies that they *do* speak it, some more, others less, according as occasion calls for its use. The general conclusion to be drawn from Mr. Ravenstein's estimate is this—that in 1879, 20·8 per cent. of the population spoke only Welsh, 33·8 per cent. only English, and the remaining 45·4 per cent. both Welsh and English. The distribution of the languages is roughly as follows:— English prevails throughout a band of varying width along the border, including the whole of Radnorshire and the greater part of Monmouthshire; along the southern seaboard, particularly in Gower and South Pembrokeshire; and to a considerable extent along the northern seaboard. Welsh is predominant in the six interior counties with such exceptions as we have noticed. A strong indication of its predominance in these is furnished by Mr. Ravenstein's computation that nearly two-thirds of the monoglot Welsh live in them. It will hardly have escaped the observation of the reader that the area of the predominance of Welsh is also the area of the marked predominance of Nonconformity. Another point deserves attention: as the two languages have in certain quarters their separate areas, we may speak of a "border" between them; but we ought in such a case to make it clear in what sense we use the term. Mr. Osborne Morgan seems to us not to have taken this precaution in his recent article in the *Nineteenth Century*, where he speaks of the churches of Wales as presenting an aspect of emptiness and desolation "as soon as the border is crossed." By way of illustrating his meaning he supposes a traveller to start from some point on the north coast (which he excludes from his remarks as being occupied by English colonies) and to strike into the interior, where he will find the churches half empty. What, then, is the border of which Mr. Morgan is

speaking? Evidently the linguistic border, and not the
political border between England and Wales. We arrive
at this conclusion, not only from the illustration which he
has used, but from the undoubted fact that for the greater
part of the political border no difference whatever can be
discerned in the size of the congregations on the English and
Welsh sides; yet nine readers out of ten would infer that
Mr. Morgan intended to represent the whole of Wales as
included in his description. Throughout his article he
ignores the work of the Church in the districts where it is
strongest—in this agreeing with Mr. Dillwyn, who excepts
from the "Welsh people," whose interests he accuses the
Church of not having promoted, Church adherents in general,
and all places in which the English language predominates.
We do not recognise the justice of this. The linguistic difficulty has been the misfortune, not the fault, of the Church,
which is bound to minister to all within the border of Wales,
whatever be the language they speak.

Sect. 2.—Reverting to the subject of Church adherents,
we have stated our belief that the proportion which they
bear to the population was arbitrarily settled long before
Mr. Dillwyn or Dr. Rees entered on their calculations. The
same may be said as to the proportion they bear to Nonconformists; for this is another mode of exhibiting the depression of the Church; and the two modes are used indifferently,
so as to become somewhat puzzling to the public, and even
(as it would seem) to Liberationists themselves. The late
Dr. Rees, for instance, having in 1884 proved to his own
satisfaction that Churchmen formed a seventh part of the
population, a few months afterwards stated at Bridgwater that
Churchmen were to Nonconformists as one in nine, adding
that this was a liberal estimate for them. It did not seem
to have occurred to him that the two statements are absolutely irreconcilable with one another; for if Churchmen
are both one-seventh of the population and one-eighth of

Nonconformists, it follows that Nonconformists are more than the whole population. But Welsh Liberationists are seldom staggered by these trifling impossibilities, and they have long since learnt the value of hardy and persistent assertion. At what date these proportions were first decided we are unable to state ; we can trace it back as far as the year 1846, when Mr. (afterwards Sir) Hugh Owen undertook a private census extending over 392 parishes, and announced as the result that the proportion of Churchmen to Dissenters was as one to eight. In 1851 this proportion was decisively upset by the Religious Census which, in spite of the abnormally high returns on the Dissenting side, showed a proportion of 1 to 3·8 attendants at the most numerously attended services. It might have been supposed that this would have superseded Mr. Owen's proportion, but no sooner was it found that the proportion was not in accordance with their wishes than Mr. H. Richard and Dr. Rees agreed to throw it overboard and to revert to the old estimate, Dr. Rees asserting that " the proportion of Dissenters to Churchmen throughout the Principality may be put down as one to eight ; but in many of the rural and manufacturing districts the preponderance of Dissenters is much greater." *Richard, "Letters and Essays," p. 19.* The only ground alleged to justify this reversal of the verdict of the Census, unsatisfactory as it was to Churchmen, was that pressure had been put on dependents and school-children to attend church on that day. We adduce this as an illustration of the manner in which Liberationists deal with any indications of Church strength. Mr. Osborne Morgan furnishes us with a further illustration of the same tendency. Referring to attendance at Church, he says :— *Nineteenth Century, 1895, p. 767.* " I put aside the large body of people who are dependent on the wealthier classes, and who naturally gravitate to the same place of worship. For in Wales, not only are most of the persons whose circumstances enable them to give employment or dispense relief to their poorer neighbours,

members of the Church of England, but the administration
of local charities is almost exclusively in the hands of the
clergy." We say nothing as to the slur cast equally on
clergy and laity—the former as bribing, the latter as willing
to be bribed—nor again as to the inconsistency of this double
accusation with Mr. Morgan's own admission that the doles
are "in most cases fairly and impartially distributed"—
what we wish to remark is the determination not to allow
the Church credit for any measure of success it may have to
show. If any of the labouring class are found inside a
church they are stigmatised as "paupers" looking out for
the loaves and fishes, and therefore to be set down as *nil* in
the estimate of Church strength.

Sect. 3.—The plea put forth by Liberationists in apology
for their method of settling the number of Churchmen in
Wales, is that the Church has not furnished any official
statement of its own on the subject. This is perfectly true ,
and the Church is wise in refraining from doing so, inasmuch as it would be impossible to produce statistics that
would be conclusive. No doubt, the Church might furnish
lists of communicants, though experience has shown that
it is by no means easy to attain correctness even in this
particular. But there is a wide step between communicants
and adherents : the latter must be to a great extent a
matter of computation, and the ratio that the one of these
bodies bears to the other is a variable one even in different parts of the same religious community, and still
more as between different communities. The outer fringe of
occasional worshippers is larger at church than at chapel,
and even outside that fringe the Church extends her ministrations, and can claim credit for the work she does in what
is termed the non-religious class. It suits the purpose of
Nonconformity in measuring itself against the Church to
treat this unfortunate section of our countrymen as though
it were non-existent. We cannot agree with this view, and

decline to have the Church's work valued simply by the number who habitually worship within the walls of its buildings. But while the Church puts forth no formal estimate of its adherents, it nevertheless furnishes indications which would enable Liberationists to test the soundness of the estimates they put forth on its behalf. Mr. Dillwyn, in his speech at Swansea, said that he had examined the charge then recently delivered by the Bishop of St. David's without finding the information he needed. Yet, if he had looked a little more closely he would have found sufficient material for throwing doubt on his own estimate of 142,639 as the number of Church people in Wales proper down to the age of four years. The diocese of St. David's contains more than a third of the population of Wales, and the section of population which would fall to its lot under Mr. Dillwyn's estimate would be about 55,000, or, accepting his exaggerated ratio for children under four, about 62,500. Now the annual number of baptisms that should take place in a population of that amount would be (if we have rightly calculated them) 2,375; but the number reported by the Bishop was 4,884. The annual number of confirmation candidates would be 1,250; but the number reported by the Bishop was 2,439. The number of communicants taken at 25 per cent. would be 15,625, but the returns of the clergy gave them as 33,560. The number of scholars should not, according to Mr. Dillwyn's estimate, exceed 11,500; but the clergy returned the average attendance at 23,108. And while Mr. Dillwyn affirmed that if the rich and the English-speaking people left Wales there would be no Church left in it, the Bishop reported that the highest return of communicants came from the most Welshy county in his diocese—Cardiganshire. Now, unless Mr. Dillwyn is prepared to say that Church returns are worthless, we do not see how he is to evade the conclusion that he has fully halved the number of Church

c

adherents in the diocese of St. David's. And in suggesting
this correction of his estimate, we do not take into account
occasional worshippers or nominal adherents. The value of
the returns may undoubtedly vary, and in all cases their
effect may be disputed by unfriendly critics. The baptisms
are registered; the confirmation candidates are provided
with tickets handed to the Bishop, who may be depended
on for correct enumeration of them. As far as the figures
go, such returns are indisputable, and their effect can only
be modified by assuming that the participants may be
members of Dissenting families. This may be possible,
though such cases can hardly be so numerous as to mate-
rially affect the value of the indication; and even these
may be adduced as evidence that the hereditary attachment to the Church's ordinances has not died out among
the Nonconformists of Wales. The same interpretation
might be, with more reason, put on the returns of marriages, the correctness of which is not open to question:
four marriages are solemnised at church for every three at
chapel, and for every seven at chapel and register office
jointly. Assume that the latter place is frequented only by
Nonconformists for that purpose, there still remains a proportion on the side of the Church which, if not accepted
as an indication of Church strength, must be accepted as
an indication of Church attachment on the part of a large
number of Nonconformists. The same observation must
be made in respect to burials: it may be said that there
is an unwillingness on the part of Nonconformists to avail
themselves as fully as they might of the Burials Amend-
ment Act of 1880 in regard to the old churchyards; but
we should be content to rest our case on the burials in
public cemeteries, where no such feeling finds place. We
might further refer to the number of scholars in Church
schools, and in this respect we should certainly claim for
the Church the credit of having " promoted the interests

of the Welsh people," and of having ministered sound religious knowledge to large numbers who do not otherwise avail themselves of its ministrations. Although the train of events has been unfavourable to the maintenance of voluntary schools in country parishes, the Church still educates about three-eighths * of the whole number now attending public elementary schools in Wales and Monmouthshire; and though many of these children belong to Nonconformist families, we are not aware of any lack of cordiality between the parents and the managers; we believe, on the other hand, that gratitude is felt by the majority of them for the stand the Church has made in defence of religious education. With regard to intermediate education it behoves us to speak with caution when we take the number of scholars as an indication of Church strength. The proportion in the endowed schools is two-thirds Churchmen to one-third Dissenters. But it has been loudly asserted that this proportion would have been greatly modified if the Dissenters were not deterred from frequenting these schools by the dread of Church influence. We cannot refrain from an expression of regret that the Departmental Committee, appointed in 1880 to enquire into the general question and into this allegation in particular, did not take more pains to ascertain what proportion ought to have existed between Churchmen and Nonconformists in these schools. They asked for returns from all intermediate schools, proprietary and private as well as endowed, but they did not apparently press for replies, nor do they refer, in connection with the denominational question, to the effect of the replies they received. The number of scholars of both sexes in respect to whom the religious profession was stated amounted to about 6,000, and of these one-half were Church adherents. A considerable proportion of that

* 108,245 on the books, 78,483 in average attendance.

number belonged to the lower section of the middle class,
which is generally admitted to have a greater tendency to
Nonconformity than the upper section. If the general average of Churchmen throughout the whole of the middle
class was such as is suggested by these returns, is there
anything abnormal in the proportion which existed among
the 1,540 boys of the upper middle class attending the
endowed schools? With all deference to the Committee,
we think that more attention should have been paid to this
point, before they accepted, as they have done in their
report, an explanation which has been largely prejudicial
to the Church. The information which they might have
obtained if they had been earnest in seeking for it, would
have thrown great light on the subject of this essay. There
is yet one criterion of Church strength to which we advert
with reluctance and diffidence — with reluctance because,
speaking for himself personally, the author has no wish to
identify the Church with any political party, and with diffidence because the criterion is one that is subject to many
qualifying considerations in connection with our subject—
we refer to the late general election, and we justify our
reference to it on the ground that Liberalism in Wales is
identified with and, we may almost say, absorbed in Liberationism. Whether the Church is identified with Conservatism in an equal degree is a question to which we should
hesitate to give an affirmative reply: Church Liberals
are probably more numerous in Welsh constituencies than
Nonconformist Conservatives. However, without going
into a discussion on this point, we may safely assert that
the Liberal party identified themselves with Liberation in
the recent election and identified Conservatism with Church
Defence. There were contests in 29 out of 33 constituencies
in the Welsh counties, and in the contested seats the proportion of Conservative to Liberal voters was as two to
three. Now we are well aware of the various elements of

See Appen-
dix B, p. 80.

uncertainty which attend any transfer of this proportion to the numbers of Churchmen and Nonconformists; but after making every allowance for abatements on the score of the four uncontested seats which were very largely Liberal, the absentee voters, the unenfranchised, and the Roman Catholics —all of them unknown quantities, as to which each person must form his own judgment—we still think that the number of votes cast on the two sides is absolutely inconsistent with such a degree of weakness as is attributed to the Church; and this conclusion appears to have been recognised by Nonconformists themselves, if we may judge by the following passage extracted from a letter in the Welsh *Tyst* as reported in the *Western Mail* of January 27 last :—" The number who voted for the Liberal candidates is not what the Nonconformists expected, and the Tory candidates polled much more than we had given them credit for. We contended before the election that Churchmen numbered only one in seven of the population, some said only one in nine. But if we take the voting returns as proofs of the relative strength of Churchmen and Nonconformists, Churchmen must constitute one-third of the population. How are we to account for it? I cannot profess to give a satisfactory answer. It cannot be denied that many Nonconformists voted for the Tories—more than we are willing to admit." Yet Mr. Richard, with characteristic persistency, says in his Essay on *Disestablishment*, published in the "Imperial Parliament" series since the election :—" It is a moderate estimate that makes the average relative proportion as six Dissenters to one Churchman."

SECT. 4.—After all that has been said, it may be objected that we have not stated the number of Churchmen in Wales. We admit it, and plead in excuse that there are no materials at hand for making more than a rough guess, which we are not disposed to do. The only possible method of ascertaining the number either of Churchmen or Dissenters is by an exhaustive official enumeration of the whole population. As to Dr. Rees's calculation of 1,100,000 Nonconformists, we have shown that it is the outcome, not of enumeration, but of guess-work and palpable errors: and the same may be said of his calculation of 224,000 Churchmen, which hinges entirely on the correctness of his calculation of Nonconformists. If we were called upon to explain to English Churchmen the position of the Church in Wales, we might do so by comparison with the Church in England. Going back to the census of 1851, we should show that the Church in Wales was on a level (as far as can be judged by returns of attendance at church) with the Church in that part of England which most closely approximates to it in natural features and in the character of its population, viz.: the Northern counties, comprising Northumberland, Durham (which answers to our coalfield), Cumberland, and Westmoreland—that it was above the Church in the great manufacturing districts of Lancashire and the West Riding of Yorkshire—considerably below the Church in the agricultural dioceses—and below the general average of the country by about 33 per cent.; that is to say, that for every three Churchmen in the whole country, there were only two in Wales. Coming to the present time, and taking the returns of confirmations as a point of comparison, it might be shown that Wales is above some of the heavier dioceses (Manchester, Durham, and Worcester), on a par with London, very much below the purely agricultural dioceses, and below the general average by the same degree as in 1851. At the same time, we should warn our interrogator that the proportions thus ascertained do not serve to fix the positions relative to Nonconformity in the two countries, for the simple reason that the population in Wales is more worked up among the several bodies than in England. The comparison with England may, however, be adduced as evidence that the Church in Wales has made progress

within the last 30 years almost, if not altogether, in an
equal degree with her more fortunately situated sister in
England. And we draw attention to this feature inasmuch
as Mr. Osborne Morgan seems to deny that any progress at
all has been made. Such, at all events, is the impression
produced by his statements, though he does not say so in so
many words. Yet, if our returns are to be trusted, the
Church is making rapid progress. Let anyone compare the
returns of confirmations for the last 10 or 12 years. We
find an increase of 51 per cent. in Bangor diocese in the
earlier as compared with the later years, 55 per cent. in
St. David's, 28 per cent. in St. Asaph, and 85 per cent. in
Llandaff. This remarkable advance is not absolutely inconsistent with Mr. Morgan's statement, that in spite of all
the zeal and energy that has been shown, "the relative
numbers of Churchmen and Dissenters have not sensibly
varied," for it is, of course, possible that Dissent may have
progressed *pari passu* with the Church in its inroads on the
irreligious section of the community. But we certainly
think that the facts we have adduced go far to contradict
what Mr. Morgan assumes to be "a fact"—that the clergy
"preach for the most part to empty churches and to deaf
ears." An ungenerous spirit of studied depreciation per-
vades the whole of Mr. Morgan's article.

Sect. 5.—A further reason for declining to make a
numerical statement of the Church strength may be found
in the extremely irregular distribution of its forces throughout the Principality. To such an extent does this proceed,
that probably Churchmen themselves would not agree to fix
on any definite amount; what would appear too high to one
person would appear too low to another, and *vice versâ*,
according as each judges by the quarter with which he is
best acquainted. The census of 1851 may be cited in illustration of this. Taking the total attendances as a point of
comparison, it can be shown that one-half of the population

contributed twice the number of attendances that the other
did, and that the percentages of attendance to population
varied from above 35 to below 5. The percentages further
enable us to define, with fair exactness, two great areas of
depression in the Church, viz., the coalfield in South Wales,
with its dependent sea-ports, and the interior counties of
North Wales comprised in the diocese of Bangor. This
two-fold depression forms the counterpart of the marked
predominance of Dissent in the two divisions of Wales, and
in each case the causes that have produced it have been
similar, though acting under widely different conditions.
The South Wales coalfield presents the difficulty arising
out of a rapid aggregation of population in a district where
the Church was unprovided with the means, as far as its
endowments are concerned, of meeting it. The interior
counties of North Wales have suffered in special localities
from the same cause, though not to the same extent : other
causes have been at work in them, particularly the extreme
paucity of clergy in by-gone years as compared generally
with the area, and occasionally with the population—a
paucity accompanied, for the most part, with a corresponding
paucity of churches, and which further contributed to
neutralise the benefits that should have accrued from the
comparative abundance of churches to be found in some
quarters. We cannot here enter into details as regards
either of these areas of depression ; but we hope to do so in
a subsequent portion of this essay. Our present purpose is
to draw attention to the fact, rather than to the explanation
of the fact. Liberationists have not failed to avail themselves of the opening thus afforded them of exhibiting the
weakness of the Church in Wales. We have a sample of
this in the one-sided attendance censuses which they have
forced upon the Church in localities where it is notoriously
weak in comparison with Dissent—at Swansea and its
adjacent parishes, for instance, where a population exceeding

100,000 has gathered in four original parishes, the endowments of which a half-century back yielded £716 a-year—in the Rhondda Valley, where a population of 55,000 in 1881, and now probably much larger, has settled on an area within which there existed, in 1831, but the single Church (originally a Chapel-of-ease) of Ystrad-y-fodwg, with an income of £85 a-year, serving for a sparse population of 1,047 scattered over an area of 16 miles in length with a surface of 24,500 acres—and, lastly, in certain groups of country parishes in the interior counties. As regards the two former districts, we are by no means disposed to exonerate the Church from the charge of tardiness in attempting to meet the emergency that has arisen. The parochial system, admirable as it is in many respects, is too stiff, and the operations of the Church, though solid, too ponderous for such cases. While the Church is making its preparations, Nonconformity steps in with its free methods, unhampered by law or traditional usages, and pre-occupies the ground. We commend its readiness, and are perfectly ready to acknowledge its services to the cause of religion, morality, and order. But we cannot, on that account, recognise the fairness of the use it has made of its advantages. The whole system of attendance censuses is unfair. Churchmen abhor the idea of converting God's house into a polling-booth and God's service into the occasion of a political gathering for polemical purposes; they cannot, therefore, enter into the spirit of the proceeding with the heartiness which animates Liberationists. The one-sided execution of such a measure is a further source of unfairness. Neither at Swansea nor in the Rhondda was the enumeration of the places of worship belonging to the Church complete,* and it was confidently asserted in

---

* Early services were not taken into account, and at Swansea three places were not visited at all by the enumerators.

the former case that it was not correct. But the most
signal unfairness consists in the use made of the figures
obtained by means of these censuses. They have been
paraded before the country by Liberationist orators in a
form which would convey the impression that they were
fair samples of the condition of the Church generally. This
is done by using vague expressions, such as the following,
extracted from the address of the Rev. J. Jones, to the
Baptist Union at Swansea:—"In *some* parishes the proportion of Nonconformists to Churchmen is as 13 to 1, in
others as 12 to 1, and in *other districts* as 10 to 1;" these
proportions apparently referring to the outlying parishes
adjacent to Swansea, while no mention is made of the
proportion of $3\frac{1}{2}$ to 1 in Swansea proper, with its 60,000
inhabitants, nor yet to the proportion of $1\frac{1}{2}$ to 1 in
St. Thomas's parish. A still larger degree of unfairness attaches to the practice of "surprise" censuses,
undertaken by anonymous and irresponsible persons, in
localities favourable for such an operation—a proceeding
which (it is needless to say) might be retorted with
effect by Churchmen, if they were minded to resort to
such questionable tactics. The returns so obtained, if
extended to chapels as well as churches, show that the
"surprise" was one-sided. In no other way can we account
for the fact, that in a small parish with a population of 300
the Nonconformist attendances reached the imposing amount
of 1,055. In another census, a person unknown professes to
give a return of attendants at 12 churches morning and
evening. In nine cases asterisks occupy the place of the
numbers, and these are explained to mean that "the
attendance was not ascertained; in some, services were not
held." In two cases the attendance is returned as *nil*. In
only two cases are the attendances at both services recorded,
and the oddest part of the thing is, that in one of these the
attendance was precisely the same (a round number) at

both services, the total attendance representing a proportion of 18 per cent. to the population, while the remainder of the group yields only 2 per cent. It never seems to have occurred to the enumerator that some explanation of this remarkable discrepancy was needed. In yet another case, the writer professes to have ascertained the number of communicants in a group of parishes, and he has reduced them from 62 (an exceptionally small number for the population) to 10. No doubt there are parishes where the Church has been well-nigh superseded by Nonconformity, and we are not prepared to say that Mr. Morgan's description of the state of the churches cannot be verified in some parts of Wales. What we complain of is that such prominency should be given to these instances as to convey the impression that they hold good with regard to all Wales. The variations are most strongly marked; they exist, not only between the border counties and the interior counties, not only between the English-speaking and the Welsh-speaking areas, but also between the town and the country parishes in both of those areas, and between different portions of the Welsh-speaking area. To strike an average between them so as to name the number of Churchmen, we hold to be impossible.

SECT. 6.—We now turn to another topic which occupies a conspicuous place in Liberationist attacks on the Church, namely, a comparison between the number of chapels and churches in Wales. It will assist the reader in forming a judgment on this matter if we state beforehand the proportion which church accommodation ought to bear to the population. It used to be said that there should be sittings for a third of the population, and assuming that the places of worship were conveniently situated and that the sittings were fairly at the service of the parishioners, such a proportion would, under ordinary circumstances, prove sufficient. Large as was the attendance on Census Day in 1851, the

highest percentage of simultaneous presence did not exceed
26 per cent. throughout the country at large, nor 35 per
cent. even in Wales ; or if we take the higher percentage of
the numbers present at the most numerously attended
services, the attendance amounted to 36 in the country
generally and 52 in Wales. It was, however, estimated by
Mr. Horace Mann that 58 per cent. might, as a matter of
possibility, be present simultaneously, and it was therefore
somewhat unnecessarily assumed that provision should be
made for that number, though it is perfectly certain that it
would never be actually required, inasmuch as many persons
are either irregular worshippers or non-worshippers. But
granting that some excess of accommodation above the
actual number of attendants is desirable, why should it be a
boast of Nonconformists that they have supplied a vast
number of sittings that cannot by any possibility be required ? And why should it be constantly cast in the teeth
of Churchmen in Wales that they have not committed a
similar folly ? The multiplicity of chapels in Wales is a
sign, not of the strength, but of the weakness of Dissent. It
has its origin in the internal rivalries of the sects, and its
effect in the struggle for congregations and in the load of
debt which now oppresses Welsh Nonconformity. What
the present accommodation in the chapels amounts to we are
not informed ; but Liberationists never cease to remind the
public that in 1851, when the chapels numbered 2,805 for
the Welsh counties, they furnished more than 680,000
sittings, making, in conjunction with the provision supplied
by the Church and the Roman Catholics, a surplusage of
cent. per cent. above what was demanded for simultaneous
use even on the Census day. The most glaring cases of surplusage are given in Table I. (p. 296) of the Census Report,
where 25 of the Welsh Registration Districts figure with
accommodation varying from 123 per cent. to 92 per cent.
of the population. The chapels are now said to number

4,361,* some of which, however, are located in England : the
accommodation is not stated, but as the modern chapels are
generally built on a larger scale than the earlier ones, we have
no difficulty in accepting the statement frequently made that
if every church were swept away, there would be plenty of
room to accommodate Churchmen in the chapels.   How this
is to be reconciled with Mr. Osborne Morgan's description of
the chapels as filled " to suffocation," we cannot understand.
If he is speaking of the counties of Denbigh and Flint, it
would be easy to show that as far back as 1851 there was
accommodation sufficient for the requirements of the population as it now stands in 1886, and we presume that chapel-
building has not been at a stand-still during those 35 years.
Possibly, however, the expression " to suffocation " is only
intended to heighten by contrast the desolate condition which
he ascribes to the churches.   We assume that the accommodation has advanced at no less a ratio than the number of
the chapels.   However this may be, the comparison now-a-
days runs between the number and not the capacity of
chapels and churches respectively.   We cannot think such a
comparison conclusive as a ground of condemnation of the
Church.   A parish church may offer accommodation equal
to two or three chapels jointly, and therefore the capacity as
well as the number of buildings should be taken into account.
Still more should the question be asked whether the accommodation furnished by the chapels is really required.   If not,
the surplusage should be knocked off before any comparison
is instituted.   Having said thus much in deprecation of the
unfair use made of the chapel argument, we are ready to
acknowledge that in so far as the Church has failed to provide adequate accommodation, it is open to hostile criticism ;
and it has failed to provide it, though not to the extent that

---

* The number licensed for marriages is 1,465 for the Welsh Counties
Division : the number registered for religious worship is 2,425.

its opponents would have the world believe. In 1851 its
buildings numbered about 1,140, affording accommodation
for about 26 per cent. of the population : but this accommodation was unequally distributed over the country, some
districts being fairly provided for, while others were left in
comparative destitution either through the shifting or through
the rapid growth of the population ; some of it, again,
was wasted through uneconomical arrangement, and some
scantily used in consequence of the unreasonable size of
the parishes. The deficiency of accommodation as compared
with the population was not, however, so baneful as the
deficiency of churches as compared with area. Since that
time a vast deal has been done to reduce the deficiency : the old
churches have been re-arranged and, in numerous cases,
enlarged : the buildings (school-churches and licensed school-
rooms included) have advanced from 172 to 273 in St. Asaph
diocese; from 198 to 241 in Bangor diocese; from 282 to
397 in Llandaff diocese ; and from 485 to 579 in St. David's
diocese. If these additions have not sufficed (and we fear
that in many parts they have not) to bring Church accommodation up to the requirements of the population, they have
at all events done wonders towards reducing the areas which
each building is designed to serve, and have brought the
Church nearer to the homes of the people. Efforts are
now being made in Llandaff diocese to increase the supply
in the coalfield ; and in St. David's diocese to do the same
in the Swansea District, which is its weakest point in
this respect. What are the deficiencies still existing, might
be ascertained by an examination of each parish ; but a
general return would fail to show. Such is the present position of affairs and, whatever remains to be done in the future,
there has been no lack of vigour or liberality in what has
been done in the past. Mr. Osborne Morgan refuses to
regard such work as any indication of progress. "The
churches are built with the cheques of the wealthy," and

therefore furnish no evidence of growing popularity towards the Church. We question the truth of his assertion; and we should be quite willing to accept the use made of the added and restored churches as a criterion of the progress of the Church in Wales.

SECT. 7.—One point yet remains to be touched upon, namely, the supply and distribution of the clergy. The number is returned in the Census of 1881 as 1,434, but this applies to the Welsh Counties Division, which has a somewhat larger area than the thirteen counties : it also includes retired clergy. The number actually at work in the four dioceses we reckon at 1,336. Comparing this with that of the incumbents and assistant curates in 1831, as given in the Report on Ecclesiastical Revenues, we find the number nearly doubled (700, as nearly as we can ascertain, at the earlier period), and there is a still more gratifying advance in the number who are resident or, if not technically resident, are engaged in attending to their parishes. Non-residence in Wales, as elsewhere, has been reduced to a *minimum.* The distribution is not so satisfactory. The Bishop of Llandaff illustrates the inequality of the distribution in his own diocese by stating in his primary charge (p. 17) that 200 of his clergy are ministering to 50,000 people while the remaining 200 are ministering to 650,000. A further comparison may be instituted between the numbers and distribution of clergy and Nonconformist ministers, the latter numbering 1,862, as compared with the above-mentioned 1,434. The most striking inequality occurs in the Rhondda District, where clergy and ministers number 10 and 60 respectively; then follow Swansea District with 20 and 56, and Cardiff District with 23 and 41. In the remainder of Glamorgan the ministers largely predominate, 370 to 212 clergy ; so also in Carmarthen, 162 to 94 in Merioneth, 104 to 64 ; in Carnarvon, 188 to 135 ; and in Anglesea, 63 to 40. In Flint, Denbigh, Montgomery, and

Monmouth they are as nearly as possible on an equality.   In
Radnor, Brecon, and Pembroke the clergy are in a slight
majority.   The proportions accord with, and to a certain
extent help to explain, the varying distribution of the two
bodies.

CHAPTER III.

SECT. 1. Causes of Church depression in Wales. The effects of the bi-lingual difficulty in Church ministrations.—SECT. 2. Collateral effects of the juxtaposition of the Welsh and English languages on the clergy, on the press, &c.—SECT. 3. Inadequacy of Church equipment in men and buildings.—SECT. 4. State of endowments at various periods.—SECT. 5. Unequal distribution of endowments. —SECT 6. Instances of districts exceptionally poor in endowments. —SECT. 7. Subsidiary causes.

SECT. 1.—The general effect of the long and (we fear) wearisome statistical discussion which has occupied the two preceding chapters, has been to show that the Church's depression has been grossly exaggerated. At the same time, we have never attempted to deny that depression exists in varying degrees throughout the whole of Wales, and especially in two areas—the coalfield of South Wales, and the interior or western counties of North Wales. The arduous task lies before us of attempting to point out the causes which have led to this depression, and to this we now address ourselves. It would be a mistake to attribute to it any single cause; it is really the result of a combination of causes, acting with varying degrees of force in various localities and at various periods of the Church's history. Of these causes two stand forth with great prominence: (1) the inadequacy, at all times and in all parts, cf the Church's equipment, and (2) the linguistic condition of Wales. It is difficult to decide which of these two has been the most influential; but we shall give precedence to the latter, inasmuch as it is the one which has pressed with exceptional severity on the Church in Wales. The Church

in England knows nothing of it; Nonconformity in Wales
has also known little of it hitherto, and has attained its
present volume very much, as we believe, through its comparative immunity from it.* We find it difficult to convey
to our English neighbours an adequate impression of the
ways in which the linguistic difficulty has worked to the
prejudice of the Church. It is tolerably well known that
Welsh is not the fireside language of the native Welsh
gentry, and that, in addition to these, there is a considerable
sprinkling of English settlers, both of the upper and middle
classes, throughout the greater part of Wales. A clergyman
is called upon to provide public ministrations for such
persons, be their number more or less, in the midst of a
Welsh-speaking population. His position is a perplexing
one. As he cannot multiply himself, he must either incur
the obloquy of refusing to minister to the English-speaking
section of his parishioners, or he must divide his services as
he best can between the two sections. Either alternative is
objectionable. If the parishioners were consulted, it may
be questioned whether the Welsh-speaking people would
approve of a clergyman refusing an English service, inasmuch as the consequence might be the removal of a well-
to-do family from among their midst. Moreover, the
courtesy and genuine friendliness which form such pleasing
traits in the Welsh character, would incline them to fall in
with the wishes of an influential neighbour. The upshot of
the deliberations has generally been that the clergyman has
yielded the point—too readily, perhaps, for the most part,
for the clergy are not blameless in the matter. What
follows? The inevitable result of bi-lingualism is to place

---

* It was stated a few years since in the House of Commons by Sir
Hussey Vivian that only 36,000 Nonconformists in Wales worship in
the English language; and as the bulk of these would be located in
the English-speaking districts, there was little cause for bi-lingual
services at that time.

the parishioners on half rations (if we may use the expression) of spiritual nutriment, and no plan has yet been devised, or ever will be devised, by which the practical inconveniences and positive disadvantages attendant on bi-lingual services may be averted. Can it be a matter of wonder that the English portion of the service is irksome to the Welshman who is not touched by the language, even when he understands it, and that on very slight provocation he betakes himself to the Dissenting Chapel close by, where the full complement of preaching can be obtained in the tongue that goes home to his heart as well as to his head? The Church is, in this respect, heavily handicapped in competition with the Chapel, and the latter acquires a more thoroughly national character in the eyes of the Welsh-speaking population. So far for the practical difficulty. But the matter does not yet rest here : beyond this, there lies the subtle influence which language exercises over the human heart, carrying a man with the force of an undefined but strong current of feeling towards the quarter where his appetite can be most fully gratified. The extent of the trial may be judged of by the fact that, in 1879, no less than one-third (402 out of 1,156) of the churches in Wales were infected with bi-lingualism. As compared with the linguistic divisions of the population, this proportion seems by no means excessive, for, the percentage of bi-lingualists being 45, the percentage of bi-lingual churches is only 34, the remainder of the churches being distributed in the proportions of 39 per cent. purely English churches * to 34 per cent. English monoglots, and 27 per cent. purely Welsh churches to 21 per cent. Welsh monoglots. But the true way of looking at the matter is to assume that the great

"Swansea Church Congress Report," p. 251.

---

* The excess of purely English churches (it should be observed) is largely accounted for by the fact that the churches are very numerous in the English-speaking districts of Pembrokeshire, Glamorganshire, and Monmouthshire.

majority of the bi-lingualists are Welsh at heart, and even though they may be quite sufficiently versed in English to join in common prayer, or to follow a sermon in that language, they yet acknowledge the sway of Welsh alone as the language of religious and poetical sentiment, and, therefore, prefer a purely Welsh to an English or a hybrid service. Coupling, then, the bi-lingualists to the purely Welsh for the purpose of our enquiry, we conclude that there ought to be 66 per cent., or two-thirds of the churches sufficiently Welsh to satisfy the aspirations of the Welsh section, and we question whether this condition is fulfilled in the bi-lingual churches. Thus, while the proportions above stated go far to exonerate the clergy from the suspicion of wishing to denationalise the Church, they leave the practical difficulty unabated. The English element is broadly, though not deeply, disseminated over the Welsh-speaking portions of Wales, and the clergy can hardly refuse to recognise it. The only effective remedy for the evil is a double supply of churches and clergy. This is possible in the larger towns, and we believe that separate Welsh churches are satisfactorily attended; but it is impossible to furnish a double equipment of churches and clergy in the smaller towns, much less in the rural parishes. The Church in Wales may justly claim sympathy and consideration in respect to the difficulties which have been presented by this insoluble problem. She has been the victim of circumstances over which she can exercise no control. She is bound to offer her ministrations in the language "understanded of the people," and when the language "understanded" by some portion of the people differs from the language "understanded" by the remainder, she is bound to do her best to meet the wants of the minority as well as of the majority. She has done this, not always in a judicious manner, but still with a good intention. She is now rewarded for her efforts by being denounced as an "alien" Church, and the "Church of a rich minority," and her deposition from her position as a National Church is demanded on the ground that she has not "promoted the interests of the Welsh people." Not that her worst foe can accuse her of not having promoted the interests of Wales as a whole; for what could possibly be more prejudicial to those interests than to have closed the door against the English-speaking section, whether consisting of hereditary Welshmen or of English immigrants, by a refusal, on the part of the Church, to recognise their rights in the parish church? Nonconformity itself will not, we presume, deny that the Church has rendered a social and economical service to Wales in this matter, and that the advantage that she has thus rendered to the country has been done to her own great disadvantage. The day may come, and that shortly, when Nonconformity will feel the full effect of the linguistic difficulty, of which it has, thus far, only had a foretaste. That it may succeed better than the Church has succeeded in meeting it is very possible. In one important respect its path will be easier; it will never have to encounter the reproach that has fallen on the Church of being an "alien" and an "English" institution, inasmuch as the preference for the English language will have penetrated deeply into the population before the emergency arises. Nonconformists look forward with apprehension to the contingency; they are well aware that their predominance in Wales is bound up with the predominance of the Welsh language. One point we have yet to notice. It may possibly be supposed by some persons that bi-lingualism in Wales is a thing of modern date. This is not the case. It may be traced back as far as Queen Elizabeth's reign. "There is never a market-town" (writes John Penry, the Puritan) "where English is not as rife as Welsh. From Chepstow to Westchester* (the whole compass of our land) "Exhortation," p. 51.

---

* Chester, under its old title of Waste Chester.

on the sea-side they all speak English. Where Monmouth and
Radnorshire border upon the Marches they all speak English.
In Pembrokeshire no great store of Welsh." And in confirmation of this, we may cite one of the charges preferred
against Bishop Ferrar in Edward VI.'s reign, that he had
preached an English sermon at Abergwili, whereas he ought
to have preached it at Carmarthen, as being an "English
town," the distance between the two places (be it observed)
being hardly more than a mile. The distinction between
the English and Welsh-speaking sections was, locally
speaking, even more sharply drawn in those days than in
these. For three centuries bi-lingualism has been the
running sore of the Welsh Church.

Sect. 2.—Thus far we have treated the linguistic condition
of Wales as it presents itself to our observation within the
walls of the parish church. But its prejudicial influence
towards the Church by no means ceases there : it has penetrated deeply into the texture of the social condition, and is
perhaps exercising a more potent influence at the present
day than at any earlier period. From the days of the
Reformation English has been the language of education and
higher literature in Wales. In particular, it has been the
language of theological literature. No original standard
treatise on theology has ever emanated from the Welsh
press—not from any incapacity on the part of Welshmen to
deal with the subject, but for the simple reason that the
readers have not been sufficiently numerous to make the
composition of such a work remunerative. The clergy and
educated laity have found their requirements fully met in
the English language, and have had the further advantage
of thus enlarging their horizon and breathing a fresher intellectual atmosphere. This must be the inevitable result
of the juxtaposition of two languages of unequal strength.
It has been through no wish or intention on the part of the
upper classes to slight their own native language that this

has happened, but through the force of circumstances. Nevertheless it has operated in various ways to the prejudice of the Church. It has, for instance, tended to produce a weakness in the use of the Welsh language among the ranks of the clergy. This again is of no recent origin. John Penry frequently notices it: he tells us that the second* "Exhort.," lesson was "most evil read of the reader and not understood p. 11. of one among ten of the hearers," and as a remedy for this he suggests that:—"Our ministers, though never so ignorant, yet all understanding English, might easily remedy this by conferring the English† with the Welsh translation : and so where they understood not their own tongue, the English might direct them, and they their hearers. But they are far from taking this small pains. I would some of them in twenty years had learned to read Welsh at first sight." He further asks:—"Why cannot we have preach- "Equity," ing in our own tongue?" and his reply is:—"Because the p. 51. minister is not able to utter his mind in Welsh:" and that he was not here speaking of immigrant Englishmen is plain from what follows:—"He may; for we have as many words as in any vulgar tongue, and we might borrow from the Latin," clearly showing that the deficiency partly arose from the condition of the language itself, which had not yet acquired its full complement of technical terms and stamped phrases for theological purposes. Preaching in Welsh involved a greater effort than preaching in English. Griffith Jones, about the middle of the last century, inveighs against the *lazy* parsons who spent their time in idleness rather than in attending to their books, " on which account they are as

---

* The New Testament alone had then been published in Welsh.

† The Act of Elizabeth prescribed that there should be a copy of the English as well as of the Welsh Bible in each church, so that people might acquire the English language. John Penry, it will be observed, reverses the process in his suggestion that the clergy might thereby learn Welsh.

ignorant of their mother tongue as of Greek and Hebrew,
and on this account read the service and preach in English":
and Howel Harris, about the same time, speaks of the folly
of addressing "an English learned discourse to a Welsh
illiterate congregation"—a remark which has been supposed
to imply the presence of Englishmen, but which was more
probably intended for the native Welsh clergy. It may be
questioned whether, even at the present day, the tendency
does not prevail, among those who are weak in their Welsh,
to prefer English to their native tongue. But the matter
does not terminate here. The thorough Welshman (meaning
thereby one who has been brought up to the use of Welsh
as the fireside language of his home) is bound to acquire some
knowledge of English before he presents himself for Holy
Orders, and he is frequently inspired with a laudable ambition
to perfect his knowledge of a language which holds so important a place in the profession to which he has devoted himself : and thus he too, in spite of his strong predilection for
his native tongue, shows a readiness to practice his English
both inside and outside of the Church, not always to the
complete satisfaction even of the English section of his
parishioners. Then, further, the Welsh Church loses many
of her most promising sons, sometimes through an inability
to compass Welsh in a satisfactory manner, more frequently
from an ability to acquire English with such perfectness
as to place him in a position to compete with Englishmen
in their own market. The tendency to exchange the scanty
herbage of Wales for the fat pastures of England extends to
the clergy as well as the laity of Wales : we find evidence of
it, as far as the former are concerned, in Penry's recommen-
dation that preachers should be compelled to return from
England to Wales in order that the pulpits might be adequately occupied : and so it has continued to the present
day in the Church. Nonconformity, on the other hand, has
been little troubled with these weaknesses or temptations

"Exhort."
p. 54.

(call them which you please) which have so seriously affected the Church. Its ministers and people form a homogeneous whole: both are predominantly, one might almost say exclusively, Welsh in conversation, in literature, and in the range of their tastes and sympathies. Hence the success and power of its press: the laity read little else than the religious periodicals of the sect to which they happen to belong. "His religion," says Mr. O. Morgan, with great truth, "constitutes his literature." The ministers are zealous in supplying this literary *pabulum:* ministers and people are alike satisfied with the quantity and quality thereof. We do not wish to speak disparagingly of it: its power* is undoubted, and therefore it is well suited

---

* The success of the Welsh Nonconformist press is constantly adduced in evidence of the numerical weakness of the Church. There is, no doubt, much force in the comparison thus instituted; yet we cannot but think that the argument is overdriven. Two elements have to be taken into consideration; one being that the number of separate publications among the Nonconformists is mainly due to the number of separate bodies, each of which requires its own special magazines or newspapers; and the other, that these bodies are, to a great extent, local autonomies with their own party questions to discuss and ther own financial affairs to manage. The true point of comparison between the Church and Nonconformity is not the number of separate publications, but the aggregate number of copies distributed. Some four or five publications would be ample for the needs of Wales if it were a united country; its religious divisions are at the bottom of the activity of its press. Church questions in Wales are, on the other hand, largely identical with Church questions in England, and, therefore, for all English readers the English newspapers are as interesting as the Welsh ones; and this condition tends to restrict the number of copies sold, just as the former condition restricts the number of separate publications. We sympathise with the managers of the Welsh Church press in the discouragements they have encountered in the past, and trust that they may meet with a larger amount of success in the future; but we do not recognise the validity of the conclusion drawn from the comparison of the Church with the Nonconformist press. The argument leaves out of view the larger number of English readers in the Church than in Nonconformity.

to its purpose. At the same time its tendency is to contract
the interests and views into a single narrow groove, within
which zeal rushes the more impetuously by reason of the
contraction. The public life of a thorough-going Welsh
Dissenter centres in his chapel, which serves to him far wider
purposes than the church does to the Churchman, being his
political,* and to a certain extent his social, club as well
as his place of worship. In all these respects Nonconformity has a distinct advantage over the Church in Wales.
Whether the advantage is one of a healthy character, is
another question: there are many who think that the

---

* Lest it should be supposed that we are taking a prejudiced view
of Welsh Nonconformists as politicians, we will quote the language of
a supporter of their cause who, under the title of " Welsh Spectator,''
addressed a letter to the *Times*, under date April 4, 1885 :—" Wales
has not evinced in the past and probably does not possess any purely
political genius; its politics are dominated by its religious institutions;
its Liberalism and its Conservatism follow with wonderful fidelity the
line of the deep fissure which religiously and socially separates Church
and Dissent. Its genius, if not religious, is certainly sectarian and
not political.'' While recognising the faithfulness of this description
as applicable to Nonconformists, we demur to it in respect to Churchmen. We deem it to be beyond all doubt that Churchmen take a
broader look-out, and are more largely interested in *imperial*, as
distinct from *local*, politics than Nonconformists. We have no wish
that it should be otherwise ; but undoubtedly it is a disadvantage to
the Church from an electioneering point of view. While Nonconformist
ministers are the busiest and most successful of canvassers, and their
chapels the focuses of political propagandism, the clergy, with rare
exceptions, hold aloof from canvassing, and with still rarer exceptions from
converting their pulpits into political platforms. The uproar that was
raised against the clergy during the recent election for deviating ever
so slightly from their usual posture under the exceptional issues raised
affecting the interests of the Church, is at once evidence of the radical
difference between the Church and Nonconformity in this particular.
The letter of " Welsh Spectator '' is candid almost to cynicism, its
object being to demand of the Government a grateful recogni-
tion of the services rendered by Welsh Nonconformists, in a
way that accords with the local and sectarian character of their
politics.

violent political rancour of Welsh Dissent is eating into the entrails of its religious life. This, however, is not the point before us. What we contend for is that much of the depression of the Church is due to the linguistic condition of Wales—that the Church has been compelled to bear the brunt of the difficulty which that condition has imposed upon the country—that though it has been outdone by the greater solidarity and homogeneity of Dissent, it has nevertheless rendered to Wales a service which Dissent could not have rendered—and that therefore the Church deserves the sympathy and consideration of every true lover of the country. Liberationists will sneer at such a suggestion, and will fall back on the simple, and to their minds clenching, argument, "You are in a minority." Our reply is that even a minority is entitled to justice, and we see no justice whatever in a judgment which shuts out of view all the circumstances which have led to its being in a minority.

SECT. 3.—We pass on to consider the other leading difficulty which the Church in Wales has encountered, namely, the inadequacy of its means for the accomplishment of its mission. We are, of course, aware of the kind of greeting which the mere mention of this topic will receive from Liberationists. "Look (it will be said) at what Nonconformity has done! Look at the chapels it has built, the ministry it sustains, the large funds which it collects annually, and let us hear no more of your plea of poverty." Far be it from us to deny to Nonconformity the meed of liberality. But when its achievements in this department of duty are adduced to throw discredit on the Church, it seems to us a somewhat one-sided contrast, because, while it exhibits the effects of voluntaryism in Nonconformity, it leaves out of view the extent of voluntaryism in the Church. It is true that this omission is unavoidable, for the simple reason that Welsh Churchmen have never attempted to

compute, in pounds sterling, the value of Church voluntaryism. It may be possible to ascertain what has been
spent in brick and mortar for the erection of churches,
schools, and parsonages: the capitalized value of endowments might also be added, and the sums annually ex-
pended on the maintenance of fabrics and services, on
schools, and missions, and poor. But who is to estimate
the amounts which the clergy bring into the Church's
treasury by providing, oftentimes partially, sometimes
wholly, for their own maintenance and that of their families
out of their private fortunes? We have not the wish,
even if we had the power, to strike a balance between the
liberality* of the Church and that of Nonconformity. We

---

p. 766.

* The annual revenue of Nonconformity in Wales is roughly stated
at £300,000, as to which Mr. Osborne Morgan observes, that " this large
sum, exceeding considerably the whole revenue of the Church in Wales,
is drawn mainly from the poorest class of a very poor country." This
statement requires modification. By "the whole revenue," Mr. Morgan
must mean the *endowments* (amounting to about £250,000 a year for
the parochial clergy) to the omission of the voluntary contributions.
But is it fair to omit these latter from the "whole revenue," and thus
represent the Church as leaning wholly on its endowments? It has
been recently stated, on the high authority of the Committee of the
"Official Year Book," that the Church in Wales contributed £107,000
in the single department of Church extension for the year 1884, and
if to this were added what is done in the ordinary support of buildings
and services, maintenance of schools, societies and charitable institutions, and in the supplementing of deficient endowments by private
incomes, would it be out of the way to surmise that the voluntary
contributions of Churchmen (few as they are said to be) equal, if not
exceed, those of Nonconformists? But then Liberationists cut away
from the Church all credit for its voluntaryism by retorting, " You are
the wealthy, whereas we are the poorest class of a very poor country."
We doubt whether this contrast is a just one. Nonconformity numbers
among its adherents a very large proportion of the money-making, as
distinct from the land-owning, class ; no class is better able or more
disposed to be liberal than this, and it is a numerous one in Wales as
compared with the landed proprietors or the independent gentry.
Mr. Morgan indeed states that the wealthy tradesman almost always

will allow Nonconformists all the credit they claim, and we
will accept the taunt too often levelled against us for not
having done more than we have done in making up out of
our own pockets the full deficiency of Church endowments.
But our present object is to ascertain how far the shortcomings of the Church are due to a misuse or non-use of the
funds entrusted to her charge by the donors of the endowments, and how far, therefore, she deserves to be deprived
of those funds, as having proved an unworthy steward.

SECT. 4.—The patrimony of the Church in Wales must
necessarily have been small as compared with the *area* of
the country, for the simple reason that Wales contains a
large amount of uncultivable land. The effect of this is
shown in the number of unsizable parishes to be found in
Wales even at the present day. It is needless to point out
that the Church's work is much impeded wherever the population, however small, is widely scattered, and the difficulty
is more than doubled if to large area is added a large, or
even a comparatively large population. This has been the
case in many parts of Wales. Church accommodation seems
to have been adequate to the requirements of the population
down to the middle of the last century. Then came a considerable increase of population, for which the existing
accommodation was insufficient, and this, superadded to the
previous insufficiency as compared with the area, and to the
insufficiency of clergy, as will be presently shown, as compared both with area and population, proved too much for

goes to church, while the small farmer and the village shopkeeper
almost always go to chapel. We doubt whether this holds good. A
large number of the upper, as well as the lower, middle-class attend
chapel, and form the financial backbone of Dissent. We admit that
Nonconformity is liberal, and we wish that Churchmen were equally
so; it should be remembered, however, that the aggressiveness of
Nonconformity has hitherto supplied a stimulus which Churchmen
have not felt in a similar degree, and that the day may come when
that stimulus may lose much of its present force.

the Church's then resources. Perhaps we may best exhibit the scantiness of those resources by a comparison with the Church in England. Lincolnshire had, in 1851, double the number of churches, as compared with area and population, that North Wales had (a church for each 550 people and 2,700 acres in the former, 1,130 people and 5,500 acres in the latter) : and it may be presumed that its patrimony was also doubly as great. At the Religious Worship Census of 1851, North Wales supplied as many worshippers, church for church, as Lincolnshire, but, having only half the number of churches, its worshippers were also half as numerous. We shall presently have to refer to the effects of this combination of population and area in connection with the South Wales coalfield. The patrimony of the Church in Wales being thus naturally meagre, was largely reduced by the diversion of the parochial endowments to monasteries, colleges, collegiate churches, cathedrals, and other purposes. South Wales suffered, perhaps, more than North Wales from these causes. To witness the full effect of this system, we must go back to the beginning of last century. The diocese of St. David's, which covers five out of the six counties of South Wales, and penetrates into the sixth in the neighbourhood of Swansea, had no more than about £10,000 a year to distribute between its parochial clergy. The condition of the diocese at this period is vividly depicted by Dr. Saunders in his "View of the Diocese of St. David's." Anything more lamentable than the state of the clergy, the churches, and the services, it is difficult to conceive. The condition of Llandaff was not much better. The two northern dioceses were not so impoverished as regards the individual clergymen ; but this was due, not so much to a larger revenue as compared either with the area or the population, as to the fact that it was divided between a smaller number of clergy.

SECT. 5.—No great improvement in the finances of the

Church took place during the earlier half of the last century. Queen Anne's Bounty Fund subsequently rendered great service to the most impoverished benefices and chapelries of South Wales and was, no doubt, the means of saving many of the chapels from falling into ruins. In 1831, we find the revenue of the parochial clergy valued at £155,000 for the four Welsh dioceses, the average value of the benefices in St. David's being about £137, in Llandaff £177, in St. Asaph £271, and in Bangor £252. Great as is the improvement thus marked, the amount was still wholly inadequate to the requirements of the Church At the modest rate of £200 a-year, it would have provided a supply of 775 clergymen for an area of 5,000,000 acres, and a population of 904,400. The total number of clergy at that time seems to have been about 700, divided into the two classes of 635 incumbents and 65 assistant curates.* As the benefices numbered 847, there was a considerable amount of plurality; but it was, to a great extent, confined to the poorest livings, and was, thus far, a matter of necessity rather than of greed; nevertheless, its effect was highly prejudicial. Passing on a half century, to 1881, the income had grown, partly through the beneficial action of the Ecclesiastical Commission, and partly through individual liberality, with the further aid of the Bounty Fund, to £232,748, as estimated in the "Financial Reform Almanack." In addition to this, the Welsh dioceses receive grants in aid of curates' stipends in mining districts from the Ecclesiastical Commissioners, to the amount of about £9,000, making a total of (say) £242,000. We omit grants from societies as being not in any sense the product of endowments. If we were again to assume an equal division of this income between

---

* There may, however, have been an additional number of curates in sole charge; but these only took the place of non-resident incumbents.

the clergy at the rate of £200 per annum, it would suffice
for a staff of 1,210. The number, in point of fact, now
working in the four dioceses exceeds this, being in all 1,336.
But meanwhile the population has advanced from 904,401
in 1831 to 1,571,000 in 1881, and therefore, though the
public has received the full benefit of the increased funds
(for the average receipts of the individual clergyman are
less than they were at the earlier period), there is still a
large deficiency of working power in the Church. Churchmen might, no doubt, supply this deficiency by increased
liberality, but they cannot be compelled to give, and
we are at a loss to see why the Church should be made
responsible at the bar of the nation for any other funds than
those which she actually has at her command. We might
again recur to a comparison with England, in order to show
the present position of the Church in Wales in point of
equipment. It appears that, while a Welsh clergyman
has on the average very nearly the same number of people to
minister to, these people are dispersed over more than double
the amount of area; and this means, in the long run, that
the people have far less opportunity of conveniently attending church than in England. And this paucity of clergy
arises from a paucity of funds which is strictly in the proportion we have already indicated. Of course, all such
calculations must be rough, and are liable to various adjust-
ments. What we desire to insist upon is the extent to which
area has affected the position of the Church in Wales—a
point which is apt to be overlooked in favour of making
population the test of the adequacy or inadequacy of Church
equipment. Add to this another most material difference
between England and Wales, namely, bi-lingualism, which
reduces the value of ministrations by one-half in many
parishes, and we think it no exaggeration to say that
Wales is 50 per cent. below England in point of material
resources.

SECT. 6.—Thus far we have spoken of the total revenue and its proportion to the area and population of the whole country. But the distribution of Church revenues is, we all know, far from being equable: and in order to form a just idea of the difficulties of the Church in Wales, it would be necessary to study the numerous cases in which the incomes of single parishes and groups of parishes fall below the average. The South Wales coalfield presents an illustration of this on a large scale. The general character of this district in its physical and industrial aspects is pretty well known to the world at large: its ecclesiastical history is known to few who live outside its limits. Much of its area consists of mountain top, formerly tenanted by a sparse population of hill farmers: churches were few and far between, and many of them small and very scantily endowed. If, taking Merthyr Tydvil as a centre, one were to strike a circle with a radius of 10 miles, it would only embrace four original parish churches, and of these only two, Merthyr Tydvil itself and Gelligaer, fall within the limits of the coalfield. The other churches existing in that portion of the coalfield at the beginning of the present century—Aberdare, Bed-wellty, Llanwonno, Ystrad-y-fodwg, Aberystruth—were originally chapels-of-ease to mother churches lying in the lower lands, which had been converted into Perpetual Curacies under the regulations of the Bounty Board. The aggregate income of the five churches we have just mentioned amounted in 1831 to £767. This country now forms the heart of the coal and iron industries, and is occupied by a teeming population. But let us now enlarge our area so as to take in the whole of the field, together with the seaports which are dependent on it for their business—Cardiff, Swansea, Newport, and Llanelly. We can select out of this district some 20 parishes, averaging 16,000 acres in size, which together with the four seaports already men-

E

tioned, now have a population of about half a million, and for which there was no other provision in 1831 than an endowment of £5,000 a year to be divided between 32 clergymen who were ministering in an equal number of churches and chapels. We have already referred to one group of parishes within this area at Swansea, having a present population of 100,000 inhabitants concentrated in four parishes, which in 1831 possessed five churches and an aggregate income of £716 a year. We have just mentioned another group of parishes with a slightly larger income (£766) now having a population of 143,000. No one, we presume, will contend that these endowments are adequate to the present circumstances of those parishes; nor, indeed, were they adequate to their circumstances 50 years back, when population had already been accumulating for more than half a century. We justify our comparison of the present population with the endowments as they stood in 1831 on the ground that it is for the use or abuse of those endowments that the Church in Wales is primarily responsible at the bar of the nation, and we conceive that no verdict of malversation would be pronounced in reference to these funds. There is a responsibility to a higher court than that of the nation, and would that we could appeal with equal confidence to its judgment! But we cannot pretend that Churchmen are blameless for the spiritual destitution in which this important district was long left as far as they were concerned—whether the cause lay in the defective organisation of the Church, in the rigidity of her parochial system, or in the want of liberality in her individual members. Nonconformity is undoubtedly entitled to the credit of having supplied ministrations which the Church had failed to supply: yet we again say that its successes form no justification for the use which Liberationists are now making of them as a groundwork of attack upon the Church. Turning, however, to what has been done, the record is by no means a contemptible one. The 32 churches and chapels, to which we have referred as being found in 24 of the parishes in 1831, have grown into 165 places of worship, and there is no ground whatever for believing that the clergy are "preaching to empty churches and to deaf ears." Two of the districts were selected, as we have already observed, for the operations of hostile censuses on the part of Liberationists. The localities were favourable for the purpose, inasmuch as church accommodation is wholly inadequate to the population. At Swansea and the adjacent parishes 23 places of worship were reported as open for a population of 100,000: in the Rhondda Valley 13 for a population of 55,000: in neither case was the enumeration complete. In the Parish of Ystrad-y-fodwg alone, which comprises about 45,000 of the above-mentioned population, the single church we have already mentioned has multiplied into 14 places of worship, viz.: eight stone churches (including two in building), two iron churches, three school churches, and one a mission room. In neither case were the churches badly attended;* but they were few, and the results of an attendance census proved satisfactory to Liberationists as furnishing a weapon for attacking the Church. We have instanced a case of difficulty on a large scale, arising out of the insufficiency of endowments. We might extend our inquiry to other parts of Wales, with a view to show that the same difficulty has presented itself on a smaller scale in various agricultural districts. We might cite, for instance, the disaster which has befallen a group of parishes in North Cardiganshire, all of them comprised in the ancient Parish of Llanbadarn-fawr, which had an area exceeding 150,000 acres (about two-thirds the

---

* The attendances in the Swansea district were returned at 10,690; in the Rhondda at 3,140.

size of the County of Rutland), and now contains a population of 28,000: the whole tithe from this area was swept
away in Edward I.'s reign to enrich the Abbey of Vale
Royal in Cheshire, and nothing has ever been received for
the support of the churches beyond a paltry pittance of
£20 a year to the vicar of the mother church. Further
illustrations might be found in the parishes which supplied
the prebends in the collegiate churches of Llanddewi Brefi
and Abergwili—those of the former situated in Cardiganshire, and of the latter in Carmarthenshire, Breconshire,
and Radnorshire: the Church has sustained a total loss of
the former through the scandalous seizure of the collegiate
estate in Queen Elizabeth's time: the latter have, been
happily retained and have already been in part restored
to the parishes whence they were taken. Some notice should
also be taken of the deficiency in bygone years of ministrations in the interior counties of North Wales, arising, not
only from the scantiness of churches in reference to area,
See Appen-
dix C, p. 81. but in a still greater degree from the scantiness of clergy
in respect to churches, there being in 1831 less than two
clergymen for every three churches in the Counties of
Merioneth, Carnarvon, and Anglesea. It should be observed
that any excess in the number of churches over that of
the clergy means disorganisation and an inadequate supply
of public ministrations; and these defects would go far
to account for the predominance of Dissent in this part
of Wales. In the census of 1851 there was a marked
contrast in the percentages of Church attendances between
the border counties of North Wales on the one hand, and
the interior counties on the other; and this contrast runs
parallel with contrasts that might be instituted between
them as to the supply of clergy, the area, the proportion
of clergy to churches, and the revenue. But, whatever
the explanation, the fact remains that the attendance in
1851 was very low in the interior counties. They are

now the great strongholds of Dissent in Wales, and supply the abnormal number of communicants which we have had occasion to notice in a previous part of this Essay. Mr. Osborne Morgan's description of "empty churches and deaf ears" may be literally true of many a parish in these parts, in spite of the zeal of the clergy and the general improvement in the organisation of the Church. It can hardly be a matter of wonder, if it be so: it is far easier to scatter than to re-gather what has been scattered.

SECT. 7.—Having dwelt with some particularity on what we consider to be the two leading causes of Church depression in Wales, it remains for us to point out some subsidiary causes which have operated in the same direction. We may mention among these, first of all, the strong feeling which has been roused in some parts of the country through the long-continued appointment of English bishops to Welsh sees, which has been construed as an act of hostility on the part of the Government towards the language and nationality of Wales. Whether it was so intended is a point to which we shall hereafter advert: we now simply notice the fact that the impression has of late years been largely diffused, and that it has been a formidable weapon in the hands of the Church's adversaries. Apart from the question of national sentiment (which cannot wisely be disregarded in the province of religion) there has been a considerable loss of influence through the inability of such bishops to minister in the language of the country. To a warm-hearted people like the Welsh the effect of administering the rite of Confirmation through an interpreter must have been chilling in the extreme; and in the rare cases where Englishmen have acquired a fair facility in the use of the language, there is an absence of the true ring in the delivery which alone can make their utterances acceptable to a Welsh ear. A second point of some interest may be noticed in connection with the

history of Welsh Methodism. Readers on the other side
of the border may perhaps not be aware that the
true Methodism of Wales is that of Whitefield and not
of Wesley. We do not attribute this to any innate predis-
position of the Welsh towards Calvinism, but to the
accidental circumstance that the founders of Methodism,
Howel Harris and Daniel Rowlands, favoured the former
of those famous leaders. Whitefield was an Evangelist
pure and simple, and did not possess the faculty of organisation which was so strong in his compeer. He founded
no sect, and in consequence of this the Welsh Methodists
remained within the pale of the Church for a much longer
period than Wesley's followers in England. Their formal
secession, by the institution of an independent ministry,
did not take place until 1811. Thus for more than 50
years Methodism had been regarded by its own adherents,
and was to a great extent regarded by the clergy, as an
Evangelical movement within the Church, and it gathered
strength and consistency through its long association with
the Church. No feeling of antagonism dwelt in the breast
of the early Methodist; he clung with tenacity to the Church
of his baptism; and even at this day there are those (a
decreasing number, we regret to think) who have not for-
gotten "the rock whence they are hewn and the hole of the
pit whence they are digged." How far the circumstance to
which we have adverted has contributed to increase the
strength of Dissent, and to impair in an equal degree the
strength of the Church, we must leave to the judgment of
our readers. Lastly, we are bound to make the painful
admission that a certain amount of the Church's weakness
is due to the baneful influence of inefficient and unworthy
men in the ranks of her ministry. We shall revert to this
topic hereafter. Our only object in mentioning it here is
lest it be thought that we were anxious to screen the Church
by omitting to mention it among the causes which have led
to the depression of the Church in Wales.

CHAPTER IV.

Sect. 1.—The second allegation brought against the
Church in Wales is that it is an "alien" institution. It
may be difficult for the English public to appreciate the full
effect of this argument in arousing the prejudices of the
Welsh-speaking population against the Church. Suffice it
to say, that it tells with great force on those who cherish a
distorted and fanatical sentiment of patriotism, and that it
serves as a stone ever at hand to throw at the Church in the
absence of more solid accusations. It would be interesting
to know when this charge of alienism was first introduced
into the controversy. Considering that the Welsh are
credited with a firm attachment to the Church down to the
commencement of the present century, we hardly think that
such a charge could have been successfully employed until
quite recent times. But now that a large secession has
taken place, the discovery has been made that the Church
not only is not at the present time, but *never has been*, the
Church of the Welsh people, and that it has been imposed
on them from without as a consequence and token of political
subjection. A heavy responsibility attaches to those who,
for mere party purposes, seek to kindle the passions of what
has hitherto been a loyal and contented people, by the use

of arguments which really tell against other institutions besides the Church. If the Church be alien, the courts of law, the law itself, and the whole administration of public affairs, not to speak of some of the Nonconformist sects, are likewise alien. The taunt, in short, cuts at the root of the whole connection between England and Wales. Even if the elements of alienism were more substantial than they happen to be, it would seem to be more consistent with true patriotism to acquiesce in accomplished facts, than to unearth from the grave of the past bitter memories of national disasters.

SECT. 2.—Mr. H. Richard is the leading exponent of the "alien" character of the Church in Wales. His arguments will be found in his re-published "Letters and Essays," and, in a more concise form, in a letter addressed to the *Daily News*, in the early part of last year. The compiler of the "Case for Disestablishment" refers (p. 107) to him for an exhaustive treatment of the subject, and proceeds to give a *résumé* of the argument. It appears from this writer,*

---

* Though we are chiefly concerned with the historical statements in the "Case for Disestablishment," we venture to suggest to the author that in future editions it would be as well to revise the statistical statements. Why should he pronounce the *total* number of separate attendants at all the services of the Church in 1851 to be 126,471 when the census pronounces the number at the *single* service to have been 132,940 ? Is it not highly probable, if not absolutely certain, that the number of individual attendants present at the three services exceeded the number present at one service ? It is true that the compiler has the high authority of Mr. Richard for this style of computation: for while Mr. Richard states that the Nonconformists present at the single service were 490,543 (which, by the way, is a misquotation, if by Non- "Letters conformists he means "Protestant Dissenters"), he calculates the total and number of Nonconformist attendants at all the services as 13,000 Essays," fewer; thus, if we mistake not, reversing the generally received axiom p. 18. that the whole is greater than its part. It is strange that Mr. Richard should not have detected so palpable an error in the twenty years that have elapsed between the two editions of his "Letters." We may take the opportunity of further noticing a discrepancy between the number

that the Church became an alien institution from the time of Edward I.'s reign downwards. "Edward the First," he says, "compelled the people to submit, and Norman barons became the lords of the soil. The usual result followed. Norman bishops and priests accompanied the Norman barons, and the British Church, like the Saxon, became the spoil of the conquerors. All differences between the Churches of the two countries disappeared, and the Church of England became established in Wales." We should have been inclined to surmise that some typographical error had crept into the text of this remarkable account of the first appearance of Norman bishops in Wales. But the compiler has carefully barred the way against such a charitable supposition by having previously stated that the event occurred after the contest between Norman and Welshman had already gone on for some centuries. It seems, indeed, somewhat inconsistent with this view that the compiler should proceed to illustrate the abject condition of the Church after Edward I.'s reign, by quoting the well-known petition of the Welsh Princes to Pope Innocent III., about the end of the twelfth, or rather the beginning of

---

of Churchmen at the single service as given by Mr. Richard in his "Letters and Essays," and in his new essay on "Disestablishment" (p. 63), which is explained by the fact that he has transferred the computed number for *all* the services to the number at the *single* service. But to return to the Liberation Society's publication. Why should the compiler quote the Church attendants at the evening service as 39,662 on p. 113, and 30,662 on p. 114? An error of the press, it may be suggested; but not so, for in each case the figures are worked into a computation. We would further suggest that figures ought to be correctly quoted, whether the variations are of importance or not. Carelessness is the pervading characteristic of Liberationist statistics. If anyone thinks well to meddle with the Religious Census of 1851, he should take the trouble to go through the calculations necessary for completeness. No returns were received from 89 out of 1,180 churches in the Welsh counties as regards sittings, and 58 as regards attendance. Credit should have been given for this latter omission in calculating the number of Church attendants.

the thirteenth century, in which complaint is made of
English bishops having been sent into Wales. But the
compiler saw no incongruity whatever in the two parts of
his statement. He probably had good ground for anticipating that his Liberationist readers would not be particular as to dates, so long as his statement was sufficiently
pungent. In one respect we can commend the compiler
above his authority, Mr. H. Richard. He states that what
befell the British Church also befell the Saxon Church.
Mr. Richard has omitted this important consideration, and
for the following very good reason, that if he had informed
his Welsh readers that the Saxon Church was treated in
the same way as the Welsh Church, the sting of the
grievance would have been largely neutralised. What the
average Welshman believes is, that the Saxons were the
first to impose alien bishops on Wales; and Mr. Richard
rather favours this idea when he speaks in his letter of the
" masterful *Teuton* temper " having tried to subdue the
Welsh under Norman rule, and that, when they succeeded,
" *English* bishops were forced upon the Welsh Church." If
he had said that *Norman* bishops had been forced alike on
the Saxon Church and the Welsh Church, the evidence of
alienism would have fallen flat on Welsh ears; for what
constitutes the gist of the Welsh grievance, is that it is
supposed to be an exclusively Welsh one: a grievance in
common with the English Church would very much cease
to be a grievance to Welshmen. If the compiler is correct
in his assertion that " the British Church, like the Saxon,
became the spoil of the conquerors," we do not see how he is
to evade the conclusion that the Church in England is just
as much an alien institution as the Church in Wales. As
to the petition of the Welsh Princes to the Pope, its value,
as an historical document, must be measured by the fact that
the presenter of the petition, Giraldus Cambrensis, was, in
all essential points, a Norman, and that the object of the

petition was to get himself appointed to the see of St. David's. In his efforts to attain this object, he was not over particular as to the representations he made, and he therefore endorses the complaint of the princes that the bishops sent from England could not talk Welsh, though he himself was equally deficient in that qualification. In advancing these criticisms on Mr. Richard's history, we must not be supposed to be approving of the high-handed proceedings of the Norman kings towards the Church in Wales: we simply assert that these proceedings do not constitute the Church in Wales an "alien" institution. Norman bishops and Norman abbots were forced upon the Church both in England and Wales, and they were no more able to talk English than to talk Welsh. War and conquest generally carry unpleasant consequences in their train, and among such we may include (what was a very general custom of those days) the claim of the conqueror to nominate bishops whom he could trust to preside over the dioceses of a newly conquered district—a dubious proceeding for the spiritual interests of the people, but not altogether a matter of wonder, considering the important position occupied by high ecclesiastics in the councils of the nation during the Middle Ages.

SECT. 3.—Mr. Richard, however, is not satisfied with tracing back the alien character of the Church for so limited a period as seven centuries; he invites us to follow him into the Norman period, and informs us in his letter to the *Daily News*, that the "Anglo-Saxons imposed their own version of Christianity on the Welsh, and, when the British Church declined their dictation, they enforced it by fire and sword." Ecclesiastical disputes were, no doubt, settled after a roughish fashion in those times, the more so as they were frequently mixed up with political and territorial interests. There is, therefore, no antecedent improbability in such an event occurring as Mr. Richard has stated. But did it

really occur? or has Mr. Richard correctly stated the way
in which it occurred? Let it be remembered that the
British and Saxon Churches were agreed on matters of
doctrine and Church polity; they differed only on points of
ritual, and especially as to the right mode of calculating the
date of Easter. Whether this can be properly called a
different *version* of Christianity we leave to the judgment of
our readers. However, the question was hotly discussed,
because it carried with it the possible fusion of the two
neighbouring Churches into a single Church. The Saxon,
or Roman Easter, was first accepted in North Wales by
Elvod, Bishop of Bangor (A.D. 755 or 768), while South
Wales held out for the old method. It was in connection
with this internal dispute between Welshman and Welshman
that the Saxons are said to have invaded South Wales.
But it is an absurdity to suppose that this incident goes to
prove the "alien" character of the Church. Mr. Richard
evidently deems it impossible that the union or fusion of the
Saxon and British Churches could have resulted from any
other cause than brute force. The whole idea of ecclesiastical unity lies outside the range of his sympathy. It is,
therefore, not a matter of surprise that he should have left
this important factor out of consideration: otherwise, he
might have assumed the possibility of the same process
having taken place between the Churches of Wales and
England as actually took place between the several branches
of the English Church, namely, that ecclesiastical unity
preceded and paved the way for political unity. We do not
say that events actually took this course in regard to Wales.
Unfortunately the history of the Welsh Church is well-nigh
a blank during the long period of three centuries that inter-
vened between the acceptance of ritual conformity with the
Saxon Church and the first appearance of Norman Lords-
Marchers in South Wales. During this period much might
have happened, and probably did happen, towards an

approximation of the two Churches; but whether this approximation developed into unity is a question which we cannot venture to determine.

SECT. 4.—In one important particular Mr. Richard carries the question back even into pre-Saxon times. His most effective proof of alienism consists in the presence of a common title for the modern representatives of the British and Saxon Churches, or (perhaps one might better say) in the absence of a distinctive title for the Church in Wales as distinct from the Church in England—both being portions of a single body called the Church of England. This argument is skilfully used to rouse the passions of the ultra-patriotic Welshman. Mr. Richard urges it in its most pronounced form: he states in his "Letter" that the title "Church of England" imports to the minds of the present generation "traditions of repugnance and hatred from the past when England was the deadly enemy of Welsh freedom and independence"—words which strike us as being somewhat out of harmony with the wholesome advice he had a few months before given to his countrymen to "lay aside suspicions and prejudices begotten of old memories, and unite with England in heart and purpose to pursue the conquests of Christianity and civilisation." We regard the argument as a signally unfair one, because nothing is known as to the time when, or the circumstances under which, the title was extended into Wales. Possibly Mr. Richard might have discovered this much for himself if he had gone on to suggest what distinctive title the Church in Wales ought to have, or could have, consistently with historical truth. It certainly could not have been "Church of *Wales*," because "Wales" is not a Welsh, but a Saxon word; nor yet "Church of *Britain*," considering that the Welsh had ceased to occupy any more than a fraction of Britain; nor is it by any means likely that it called itself by any such title as "Eglwys Cymru": in short, as Wales was not a political unit, we cannot conceive the possibility of its Church having had *any* collective name, and we fall back on the supposition that each diocese formed a separate unit named after its Bishop's see. If this were the case, nothing would be more natural than that the title "Church of England" should extend over Wales as it had gradually extended over England, not as the result or sign of political subjection, but rather as the result and sign of ecclesiastical unity. We submit this explanation with great deference. Mr. Richard may possibly be right in his historical view, but we hold him to be morally wrong in even suggesting that the Welsh people are inspired with thoughts of "repugnance and hatred" at the name of England, in whatever connection it may be mentioned. We may, in conclusion, observe that the argument is one that may cut both ways: the Nonconformist sects are equally alien in their titles, which are all derived from England, and infinitely more alien in their origin than the Church.

SECT. 5.—From first to last Mr. Richard can find no redeeming feature in the connection that has probably existed for a thousand years between the Church in Wales and the Church in England:—"Its influence, whether hostile or friendly, whether in Catholic or Protestant times, has been uniformly disastrous." The policy of the State (according to him) has been directed to the extinction of the language and nationality of Wales through the instrumentality of the Church. He finds increasing evidence of this as time rolls on, and points to a marked change which he states in his "Letter" to have occurred at the Revolution, and which was manifested in the appointment of English Bishops to Welsh sees. Mr. Richard has adopted without enquiry the crude theory devised by the late Mr. Johnes on this subject, which was to the following effect: that in consequence of the Jacobite proclivities of the Welsh, William III. or George I. (it does not exactly appear which of the two) sent English

"Letters and Essays," p. 133.

bishops into Wales both as a punishment and as a safeguard. This theory, however, leaves out of sight the important fact that a considerable number of English bishops had been sent to fill Welsh sees from the time of Elizabeth downwards, so that in the large diocese* of St. David's there had hardly been any Welsh ones. It may be further shown that William III.'s reign was rather distinguished by the circumstance that the vacancies were filled up exclusively with Welsh bishops. Evidence may also be produced to show that the Welsh were by no means conspicuously Jacobite; so far from it, there was a large and influential party favourable to the Hanoverian† dynasty. The whole theory of hostile intent on the part of the English Government in this matter collapses under these plain facts, and it remains an open question why English bishops were sent into Wales. Circumstantial evidence points to the following solution—that in South Wales the incomes of the sees were so attenuated from the Reformation downwards as to require to be supplemented by English preferments, and this arrangement remained in force within the memory of many persons yet living, Llandaff being combined with the Deanery of St. Paul's, and St. David's with the Deanery of Durham; in North Wales, on the other hand, the Welsh Episcopate died out, through the operation of two

---

* Bishop Davies (1561-1582) was an undoubted Welshman, and so was William Thomas (1678-1683) in all respects except the place of his birth (Bristol). Thomas Young (1560-1561) may well have been connected with a family of that name settled at Nevern; but there is no evidence that this was the case. Marmaduke Middleton (1582-1594) has been reputed to be a native of Cardiganshire, but Lewis Dunn pronounces him a Yorkshire man. John Lloyd (1686) held the see only for a few months. Including the doubtful cases, the see of St. David's was occupied forty years by Welshmen from the beginning of Elizabeth's reign down to the appointment of the present incumbent.

† The annals of the "Society of Ancient Britons," located in London, bear testimony to this fact. The Society was founded in 1715 in loyalty to the House of Hanover as expressly mentioned in their minutes.

causes, namely, the promotion of the Welsh bishops to
English sees, and the transfer, in the early part of the last
century, of the selection of bishops from the Archbishop of
Canterbury to the Prime Minister, who utilized his patronage
for the promotion of party interests. Under the action of
these combined causes the Welsh episcopate became thoroughly
assimilated to the English. We do not undertake to justify
the policy: it was a bad system for the Church whether in
England or in Wales, but it was more felt in the latter country in consequence of the presence of the Welsh language.
We cannot, nevertheless, honestly discover any traces of
hostile design on the part of the English Government: as
far as South Wales is concerned we find evidence of the very
opposite intention; we therefore do not believe that the
Church derived an "alien" character in the eyes of the people from this cause, until it was suggested some half century
back that there was a deeply laid plot at the bottom of it for
the extinction of the language and nationality of Wales.
This is what Mr. Richard still believes and what he certainly
has not proved. No Prime Minister ever avowed a motive
of policy, and no Bishop ever accepted a Welsh see with the
understanding that it was part of his office to throw a damper
on Welsh nationality. The party interests taken into consideration in their selection were simply those of Whig *versus*
Tory, and not of England *versus* Wales. The English bishops
in Wales never constituted themselves leaders of an English
party after the fashion of Irish bishops of the Archbishop
Boulter type. Nor did they so far neglect their respon-
sibilities as to oppose the use of the Welsh language in
Church ministrations. We might cite the names of Bull,
Beveridge, Fleetwood, Warren and Thirlwall, in refutation of
such a charge; and possibly the list might be enlarged, if we
knew more of the doings of the bishops in past times. It is no
part of our business, however, to discuss this point farther than
as it elucidates the question of the motive of their appointment

Sect. 6.—Mr. Richard would doubtless point to the conduct of the English bishops as justifying the worst construction that can be placed on their appointment. "They inundated the Principality," he says, "with English clergymen." Now, un- doubtedly, if this were literally or even approximately true, the Church in Wales might have contracted an "alien" character in the eyes of the Welsh-speaking people. But it is simply untrue. The number of English clergymen holding Welsh-speaking livings during the last 150 years has been so small as to justify us in pronouncing such cases to be quite excep- tional: the great bulk of the clergy have been unmistakably Welsh. We are speaking (be it observed) of the *parochial* clergy; and Mr. Richard must be held to refer to these, inasmuch as he quotes in condemnation of the practice the 26th Article, which forbids ministrations "in a tongue not understanded of the people." It cannot be denied that the clergy have frequently been weak in their Welsh, so weak, indeed, as to be sometimes unfit for their posts; but it would be a mistake to conclude that these were necessarily English- men: we have already remarked that this has been a not uncommon failing of the native Welsh clergy. This, how- ever, is not the gist of Mr. Richard's accusation. What he asserted in his letter to the *Daily News*, and reiterates in his essay on "Disestablishment," is that the English Bishops inundated Wales with their English friends and relations. His assertion was challenged by the present author in his "Reply to Mr. Richard," published immediately after the "Letter." It was pointed out that in the large diocese of St. David's the family name of a Bishop was not introduced into the roll of the clergy for the 150 years succeeding 1700, and that only two collateral relations had been detected as holding parochial preferment, one of whom was located on the English border, while the other may have been in Wales before the Bishop. The Bishops of Llandaff had but two livings to dispose of in their own diocese, and we are not aware that

"L. and E.," p. 147. Mr. R.

they have ever been charged with nepotism in respect to either of them. In Bangor we may notice the presence of Dean Cotton, who, by virtue of his deanery, had parochial duties, and Mr. Majendie—both of them related to a Bishop, and neither of them sufficiently trained in the Welsh tongue to satisfy a Welsh ear. Setting aside these two, we must go back a hundred years to find any instance of an English clergyman having been even nominated to a benefice, and the man to whom we refer as then nominated, Dr. Bowles, appears never to have been actually appointed, as his name is not found either in the diocesan register as having been instituted, nor yet in the parochial register as having officiated—the explanation being that on appeal to the Court of Arches the presentation was cancelled. Further back than this, to the beginning of the 18th century, we find some English names, but in no case a Bishop's family name; and we have been unable at this distance of time to ascertain whether the bearers of those names which do occur were natives of Wales or not. Coming to St. Asaph, it cannot, unfortunately, be denied that there was at one period a scandalous display of nepotism, the particulars of which we shall detail in the next chapter; but here again the facts do not warrant Mr. Richard's sweeping accusation as to the inundation of Welsh benefices by incumbents ignorant of the language " understanded by the people." Mr. Johnes, who criticised the appointments with great severity, specifies two such cases; but in neither of these cases were the incumbents related to a Bishop, and one of them was not promoted by a Bishop. Other cases there were of English incumbents, relations of Bishops, appointed to parochial benefices in the diocese; but these were located in the border parishes, where English was the predominating language; and though it is very probable that there was a minority of Welsh-speaking people who were entitled to more consideration than they actually received, there was no very glaring impropriety in the appointments on linguistic grounds. We form our opinion, not on personal knowledge of the localities, but from the statements in Mr. Johnes' " Essay."

SECT. 7.—Whether any further elements of alienism are attributed to the Church in Wales in addition to those we have noticed, we are not fully aware. Mr. Osborne Morgan speaks of its being to the Welsh Nonconformists an alien p. 766. Church; but so might he speak of the Church in England as being alien to the English Nonconformists. We question whether the term alien is properly used in such a case. He states, indeed, that the " Welsh Celt, like his Cornish cousin, See Appendix D, p. 83 is by nature predisposed to be a Nonconformist ;" but this is hardly consistent with the fact that Welsh Methodism originally sprang out of the Church, and adhered to the Church much longer than did Methodism in England. If " alien " merely means that the Nonconformists of the present day are estranged from the Church, we must accept the statement, certainly as regards the · Congregationalists and Baptists, and, in a measure, the Calvinistic-Methodists. If, on the other hand, what is meant is that Welsh Nonconformists regard the Church as alien in the sense of being devoted to English interests, we most emphatically protest against the imputation as in the highest degree unjust. We have already expressed our conviction that the Church has suffered severely from the double duty imposed upon her of providing for both the Welsh and English elements of the population, and she is entitled to generous consideration in this respect for the difficulties she has had to meet with in this respect. We make no doubt that it has contributed to give to the Church an alien hue in the eyes of the monoglot Welshman : but it does not follow that the imputation is deserved.

CHAPTER V.

SECT. 1.—It remains for us to advert to the charges of negligence and corruption alleged against the Church in Wales. It would argue badly for our standard of duty if we were to assert that such charges are altogether without foundation. Where, indeed, is the Church, established or unestablished, which could or would pronounce itself faultless? Even Nonconformity is not perfect, though Liberationists do not hesitate to cast the first stone at the guilty. As regards the Church in Wales we do not pretend to present a *couleur de rose* description of her doings : we acknowledge a long tale of faults and shortcomings. All that we propose to do is to ask whether our assailants have been fair either in their statements of facts or in the deductions they have drawn from those facts. The charge of corruption is closely attached, in the argument of our assailants, to the charge of alienism, the contention being that the Bishops have been corrupt because they have been alien, and alien because the Church has been established. Thus, for instance, the compiler of the "Case for Disestablishment" introduces his sketch of the post-Reformation period in the following words :—" The Church of England in the Principality continued to be the Church of the stranger.

Its chief shepherds cared little for the native flock of the ecclesiastical fold. but they showed themselves intent on securing as much as possible of the fleece. In 1587 it transpired that the Bishop of Bangor held sixteen rich livings in *commendam.*" This instance of corruption is one of the stock topics in Liberationist utterances: we find it adduced in Dr. Rees's "History," in Dr. Rees's address at Swansea in 1884, in Mr. Richard's "Letters and Essays," and in his recently published handbook on "Disestablishment." We have two questions to ask on the subject of this and similar statements—the first being whether it is fair to reproduce scandals which occurred some two or three hundred years since with a view to rouse popular indignation against the Church of the present day—the other whether it is not the bounden duty of those who choose to adopt this unfair mode of attack, to use the most scrupulous caution in laying the case fully* and fairly before the public by stating the facts correctly and by placing it in a position to judge of the value of the facts by describing the character and circumstances of the period in which they occurred. We do not for a moment contend that such topics should be excluded from the pages of history. The first qualification of a historian is that he should be faithful in his description of the times with which he is dealing; but it does not follow that such subjects should be introduced into platform addresses for the unworthy purpose of rousing passion and prejudice against present institutions. And, to take our second question, we

---

* Mr. Richard does not apparently think it needful to be prepared with particulars to prove his assertions even as to events which he alleges to have occurred within the last few years. He may recall to his memory a story that he recounted at Dowlais publicly on Nov. 12, 1885, about a Nonconformist graveyard and a clergyman's conduct relating to it, which he was called upon to substantiate, but could give his interrogator no particulars whatever as to place, person, or denomination. We submit that he should yet furnish the information with such fulness as would enable a person to verify the statement.

contend that the most rigid care should be used to sift the exact character of every fact recorded and every statement made. We will illustrate our meaning by reference to the case above referred to. The Bishop in question was a thorough-going Welshman, William Hughes, not of Bangor, but of St. Asaph. Strype records, no doubt, that he held sixteen livings; but he also gives some particulars as to these livings, and those particulars ought, in our opinion, to have been mentioned. In the present day, when we hear of a clergyman holding a living, we think of him as having a rectory or vicarage, with duties attaching to the post ; but in past times there was another class of livings, called sinecures, which did not involve such duties; and these were often applied to supply funds for the maintenance of the higher officers in the Church, such as Bishops and Archdeacons. Now, Strype tells us that ten out of the sixteen "livings" were *sinecures*, and Mr. Richard ought to have mentioned this. Still, it may be said that the Bishop had no right to derive his income from these ten sinecures, much less from the six livings with cure of souls which he held. On this head it should be explained that in consequence of the then poverty of the see (valued at £187 a year), Archbishop Parker had authorised the Bishop to hold in *commendam* the Archdeaconry of St. Asaph, the Rectory of Llysfaen, which he had held before his elevation to the see, and other benefices to the value of £150 per annum. The Archdeacon's revenue arose out of three livings with cure, and four sinecures; and the Bishop further took two benefices with cure, and four sine-cure rectories with two chapelries attached, in satisfaction of the £150 a year. We have thus accounted for the sixteen livings in a very different way from what nine-tenths of Mr. Richard's readers would understand it, and we maintain that he should have taken some pains to understand it himself and to expound it to others. That the system was a bad one we freely grant; and that the Bishop created a scandal may also be taken for granted, the scandal consisting partly in this, that he shifted from time to time the benefices which he took in *commendam*, and that the livings he took exceeded in value the stipulated £150, unless this latter sum be understood as representing the value in the King's books. We have no wish whatever to whitewash Bishop Hughes's character, but we equally have no wish that the guilt of his misdoings should be transferred to the now existing Church; and, whatever that guilt may amount to, it does not prove that the Church was "the Church of the stranger."

SECT. 2.—From Bishop Hughes and his sixteen livings, we descend to more recent times and find the English Bishops depicted by Mr. Richard in his "Letter" as uniformly and universally corrupt:—"They displayed the most rapacious spirit: a system of nepotism, plurality and non-residence of the most shameful character prevailed. The highest appointments—deaneries, canonries, and some of the richest livings were bestowed by the Bishops on their own relations and friends." The importance of this charge may be judged from the fact that it has more than once supplied materials for assaults on the Welsh Church in the House of Commons, notably so in 1871, when the late Justice (then Mr.) Watkin Williams founded his motion for the Disestablishment of the Church in Wales mainly on these grounds. The authority on which both Mr. Richard and Mr. Watkin Williams relied for their statements is Johnes' Essay on the "Causes of Dissent in Wales," published in 1832. Mr. Johnes lived at a time when nepotism had attained an unfortunate notoriety in the diocese of St. Asaph, within the borders of which he lived. There was ample ground for complaint as far as that diocese was concerned, but there can be no question that the language he used was likely to mislead cursory readers of his Essay as to the extent, both in area and time, to which the grievance had extended; he conveyed the impression that the malpractices prevailed throughout the whole of Wales and in

respect to all classes of preferments that were worth having.
Even as regards St. Asaph diocese his statements are too
highly coloured, while as regards the rest of Wales they do
not apply in any marked degree. Mr. Watkin Williams
cited to the House in 1871 the terms of a petition presented
to it some 40 years before. which evidently emanated from
the diocese of St. Asaph, but which was represented as applying to the whole of the country. Great injustice has thus
been done to the Church in Wales and to the memories of the
Bishops as a body. As far as South Wales is concerned,
there is no ground whatever for the charge; it may be said,
of course, that the charge applies only to *valuable* appointments, and that there are none such in South Wales : this is
not far from the truth, but then it surely should have been
made clear that the larger division of Wales was unaffected
by the abuse. The Bishops of St. David's* however, had not
bad opportunities of promoting their friends to the higher
posts which they had to dispose of : but for the century and
half that preceded 1850 we can detect the family name of a
Bishop among the higher appointments only once. in the
person of Archdeacon Warren, nor have we been able after
diligent search to discover more than one other collateral
relation of a Bishop as holding a post of this kind, namely
Archdeacon Stevens, son-in-law of Bishop Bull. The Bishops
of Llandaff had (as already stated) hardly any parochial
preferment at their disposal and the cathedral appointments
were little else than honorary. Such as they were, they
might very possibly have been more judiciously disposed of,
but they certainly furnished no opportunity for the exercise
of "rapacity." In Bangor diocese the relations of bishops

---

* It may not be amiss to remark that in reviewing the names of the
holders of higher appointments at the disposal of Bishops, allowance
must be made for "options" and Crown appointments *sede vacante*.
In St. David's, where the succession of Bishops was very rapid, such
cases were numerous.

were not unknown. The names of Dean Warren, Dean Cotton, and Mr. Majendie have been already mentioned, and to these we may add the names of Henry Warren (1797), Henry Egerton (1758), and Egerton Leigh (1759), the two latter of which suggest connection with Bishop Egerton (1756-1769). Here our list of Bishops' relations (as far as we are able to identify them) comes to an end for a period of 180 years. It was only in St. Asaph that nepotism prevailed, and, without offering the slightest palliation for the offence, we wish, nevertheless, to state the facts of the case. The chief occasion for its exercise arose out of a dozen sinecure rectories, which, as having no parochial duties attached to them, might be held by persons living in England or elsewhere. These were largely distributed among the friends of the Bishops as shown by Mr. Johnes (p. 140), and the only complaint we have to make of his comments on these appointments is that he frequently mixes them up with the parochial cures under the common term " benefice "; whereas we think it somewhat essential to a true estimate of the effects of the appointments that they should be described as *sinecures*. Then, further, the Deanery was held by five relations of Bishops for 150 years, and very much the same may be said of the more valuable of the prebends. Lastly, four successive Bishops had left behind them relations to the number of 11, holding between them 15 parochial benefices, and these persons happened to be holding these benefices *simultaneously* when Mr. Johnes wrote, so that though the number of individuals preferred by each Bishop was not excessive, the aggregate number was certainly so, and the state of the diocese was deservedly the object of much adverse criticism. We offer no defence for the conduct of Bishop Luxmoore and his predecessors. But we still maintain that it is a gross exaggeration to say of the Welsh prelates generally that they " preferred their inefficient sons, nephews and cousins to the fourth and fifth

generation " (Johnes, p. 137), or that they "inundated " the
Principality with English clergymen. The actual number
whose positions necessarily imposed upon them intercourse
with the Welsh-speaking population, probably does not
exceed a couple of dozen for a couple of hundred years.

Sect. 3.—Mr. Richard carries on his attack from the Bishops
to the parochial clergy, whom he describes as "a most de-
generate class, utterly indifferent to their office, and many of
them leading scandalous and immoral lives." It is difficult to
deal with a vague and sweeping accusation of this sort. We
have already allowed that there have been, and still are, clergymen whose characters unfit them for their office. We are not
in a position to deny that the number of such has been pro-
portionately larger in Wales than in England. If there be any
truth in the assertion that "a scandalous maintenance makes a
scandalous ministry " (and we believe that this is accepted as
an axiom by Nonconformists equally with Churchmen), there is
good reason for anticipating, though not for justifying, a lower
standard in Wales than in England. Add to this the chilling
effects of isolation to which the Welsh clergyman is exposed in
many a remote mountain parish, and we shall still less wonder
at what has frequently happened, though it ought not to have
been so. The effect of such cases is felt widely in point of
area and long in point of time, while the memories of worthy
and faithful pastors are buried in oblivion. Never was the
saying more true than in respect to the clergy, that—

> " The evil that men do lives after them,
> The good is oft interred with their bones."

"L. and
E.," p. 144

And thus it comes to pass that Mr. Richard is enabled to quote
from the presentments to Bishop Baily, of Bangor, in 1623,
such statements as that the Vicar of Aberdaron was on a certain occasion "overseen by drinke," while nothing can be
placed on the *per contra* side of the account in the absence of
all record.

One further observation we have to make on this subject. It is frequently assumed that the rise of Methodism, both in Wales and in England, was due to notorious misconduct on the part of the clergy. Mr. Richard, in his " Letter," does not omit to avail himself of Bishop Ryle's assertion that at the time when Daniel Rowlands' license was revoked, " scores of "Christian Leaders," Welsh clergymen were shamefully neglecting their duties, and p. 103. too often were drunkards, gamblers, sportsmen, if not worse." We are as little able to disprove, as we imagine that Bishop Ryle is to prove, this vague charge. But we conceive it to be a mistake to regard this as the root of the success of Methodism. Methodism was rather a recoil from the dry, hard tone which had prevailed in theology, in the pulpit, and in the general religious tone of the day, to an excess of warmth and excitement—a violent swing of the pendulum from the intellectual to the emotional side of religion. But the dryness and hardness were quite compatible with morality and a certain kind of earnestness : and we believe that the clergy were by no means held in contempt in the early part of the last century. Methodism, after all, sprang out of the bosom of the Church— Griffith Jones, Daniel Rowlands, and many other Methodist leaders being clergymen. Howel Harris, who shares with Daniel Rowlands the fame of having founded Welsh Methodism, was a layman ; but he attributed his first religious impressions to the ministrations of his parish priest, and he remained an attached member of the Church to the end of his life.* We do not find these early readers of Methodism inveighing against

---

* These interesting facts are alluded to in the inscription on the tablet to Harris's memory in Talgarth Church :—" Near the Communion Table lie the remains of Howel Harris, Esq. Here where his body lies, he was convinced of sin, had his pardon sealed, and felt the power of Christ's precious blood, at the Holy Communion " ; and the same inscription records that he remained a " faithful member of the Church of England unto his end."

the lives of the clergy as the occasion of the movement they set on foot.

SECT. 4.—Negligence of a flagrant character is also alleged against the Church in Wales. The topic generally selected to support this charge is the delay that occurred in publishing a Welsh version of the Bible. The facts are as follow :— Queen Elizabeth ordered (A.D. 1563) the Welsh Bishops (Hereford included) to prepare a Welsh version of the Bible, and to get the same printed and published within three years, under the heavy penalty, in default, of £40 each. Not only was the time absurdly short for such a task (as may be readily concluded from the time occupied even in the *revision* of the English Bible, both in James I.'s reign and in our own time), but it was in the highest degree unreasonable to impose on the Bishops, whose incomes were insufficient for their own maintenance, the great expense of carrying such a work through the press in London : for (it must be remembered) the Queen, in ordering them to do this, never offered to find them the money wherewith to do it. The version of the New Testament was brought out in 1567; but the Old Testament not until 20 years later, and then through the assistance rendered to the translator (Morgan) by Archbishop Whitgift and Dean Goodman. The version is one of which Welshmen are justly proud ; and nothing can be more ungenerous than Mr. Richard's observations on this subject in his " Letter," dilating (as he does) on the neglect, without mentioning the difficulties of the case.

SECT. 5.—Much more might we say of the treatment, at once unjust and ungenerous, which the Church in Wales has received at the hands of those who profess to be animated with the most friendly feelings towards her, and exhibit their friendliness by exposing her shortcomings without explaining the causes of them, and by raking up all sorts of charges against her from the events of the last thousand years. Her history has, no doubt, been largely involved in and influenced by the political and social history of the country : it was impossible that it could be otherwise. Her adversaries have skilfully chosen their ground for depreciating her through this inevitable connection. Because she has been an integral portion of the Church of England—because she has shared the fortunes of that Church for good and for evil—because she has been almost exclusively responsible for the English element in the Welsh-speaking districts—and because her efficiency has been in various ways impaired by the juxtaposition of the English and Welsh languages—for these reasons she is denounced as an alien institution, and no longer worthy to be regarded as the Church of the people of Wales. We appeal to the judgment of the public, both inside and outside of Wales, to decide whether the shortcomings of the Church in Wales have not been grossly exaggerated, and her position unduly depreciated by persistent misrepresentation.

APPENDICES.

APPENDIX A.

Mr. Dillwyn has himself illustrated the fallaciousness of his statement of 1883 by his recent statement in the House of Commons, in which he reduced the proportion of children to population from one-fifth to one-sixth, and also reduced the non-religious section from 150,000 to 100,000 (children in each case excluded). The amount thus gained he has distributed between Church people and Roman Catholics, the former being raised from 142,639 to 217,400, and the latter from 30,000 to 50,000—all these figures being exclusive of children. But the true way to compare Mr. Dillwyn's two statements is by including the children, and it will be found that they stand thus:—Nonconformists are reduced from 939,930 as stated in 1883 to 902,330 as stated in 1886, and non-religious from 187,500 to 120,000; but Roman Catholics are increased from 37,500 to 60,000; leaving the balance for Churchmen increased from 178,300 to 260,900— the total population in each case being the same, 1,343,320. Sundry questions are suggested by this comparison. In the first place, how does Mr. Dillwyn make out the proportion of Churchmen to population as one-eighth, which was what he stated to the House?   It is clearly one-fifth, as any one may observe by comparing the two amounts last mentioned. Mr. Dillwyn made a similar miscalculation in

1883 when he stated the proportion as one-ninth though his figures showed one-seventh. Unless he can offer some explanation of these discrepancies, he is certainly open to the charge of culpable mis-representation. Then, further, how does he account for the changes he has introduced into the later as compared with the earlier estimate? He has advanced Churchmen to the extent of 82,600 of the population, about 50 per cent. of their former number, and Roman Catholics 22,500 or 60 per cent., and he has diminished the children by 44,800, and the non-religious by 67,500. Does he mean to say that such changes have actually taken place within these sections during the last two years? or does he acknowledge that one of his statements is wrong and, if so, which? Meanwhile it is observable that he retains the number of Nonconformists members and hearers at the same amount as before, though it has been pointed out more than once that he has mis-quoted the returns and thus enhanced their number to the extent of about 50,000. These mistakes he certainly ought to have rectified, with the result that the proportion of Churchmen to population would have been raised from one-fifth to one-fourth, and even higher than this if he had further modified his calculation as to the children. Even thus his whole statement would labour under the radical defect of being constructed on a fallacious basis: it is simply monstrous that the number of Churchmen should be made to depend on Nonconformist returns which are not open to public inspection—yet more monstrous that it should be made to depend on arbitrary assumptions and arithmetical blunders.

APPENDIX B.

The explanation suggested by the Departmental Committee has obtained more ready acceptance at the hands of
the public in consequence of the exaggerated estimate put
forth by them as to the number of scholars that ought
to be receiving intermediate education. Mention is made
in their Report (p. 16) of 16 boys per 1,000 of the population
as being a fair proportion, and the idea has somehow got
abroad that this number is actually found in the endowed
schools of England. This impression receives confirmation
from their proposal to make provision for the reduced
number of 10 per 1,000, "on account of the exceptional conditions of Wales." The contrast between those proportions
and the one per 1,000 actually found in the schools has
naturally engendered the suspicion that there must be something radically wrong in the management of the schools
in order to account for the extreme paucity of scholars in
Wales. If the Committee had stated that the number in
the endowed schools of England was, a few years since,
only at the rate of two per thousand, or if they had made
it clear that proprietary and private schools should be taken
into account in estimating the total number receiving intermediate education, and that, as regards Wales, particular
inquiry should be made as to the number of boys receiving
such education in England, then a very different reception
would have been given to their explanation, which receives
no confirmation, but rather the reverse, from the condition
of such of the endowed schools as are not under the management of Churchmen. We are glad to be able to fortify
our view by quoting the testimony of one who can speak
with the authority of a large experience—the Rev. A. G.
Edwards, for 11 years master of a school, Llandovery, which

has been much frequented by Nonconformist boys. Addressing the Cambrian Society of South Wales and Monmouthshire at Cardiff, March 9, 1886, he says:—"I affirm positively that the statement that existing First Grade Schools are viewed with mistrust by parents on account of the religious views of those who preside over them, is a statement which does not rest on any basis of fact." And he proceeds to state that the paucity of scholars in Wales is rather due to the preference which parents show for having their sons educated in England whenever they can afford the expense.

APPENDIX C.

The paucity of clergy as compared with churches has been in past times most conspicuous in Anglesea and the peninsula of Lleyn in Carnarvonshire. In these districts old churches are far more numerous than in other parts of North Wales: whether this is due to the superior fertility of the soil or to ecclesiastical conditions we are not aware.

In Anglesea there were, in 1831, as many as 75 churches and chapels-of-ease; in Lleyn (or, more exactly, the Registration District of Pwllheli) 31 churches and chapels. These 106 buildings were divided amongst 56 benefices, so that there were nearly two churches for each benefice. This disproportion arose from two causes, one being the numerous chapels-of-ease which remained attached to the mother churches, and the other the consolidations that had taken place in consequence of insufficiency of income. The areas which the chapels-of-ease served had in many cases become recognised as civil parishes, and hence there was all the appearance of a large amount of plurality ; but plurality must be measured by the number of benefices and not by the number of churches. There were, indeed, some cases of plurality in 1831 : we could mention about · ten, five of which might be justified by the poverty of the benefices, while the remaining five cannot be justified on that ground. These latter cases would come under the head of abuse or mal-administration. But setting these aside, the number of incumbents could hardly exceed 50 under any circumstances. Curates might, of course, be added if funds permitted : but there were no more than six assistant curates in 1831. It is clearly impossible that 50 clergy can supply the full complement of services requisite for the satisfactory working of 106 churches ; this would have been the case even if all the benefices had been filled with active resident clergy, and irrespective of the abuses of non-residence and negligence which undoubtedly prevailed at that period. The general effect of the deficiencies of one kind and another is told in the low percentages which are shown by the census returns of 1851, the total attendances numbering only 7·8 per cent. of the population in Lleyn and 10·5 in Anglesea. We may particularly notice the meagre attendance in the evening, which shows that the churches were for the most part closed just when they would have had the best chance of being filled. Turning to other portions of these western counties, we find that in the Registration District of Carnarvon (excluding that portion of it which lies in Anglesea) there were in 1831 but 12 churches and chapels and 10 benefices for an area of about 95,000 acres : the percentage of attendances in 1851 stood at 8·2 for a population of about 30,000. In Festiniog there was again a disproportion of clergy to churches, there being in 1831 but nine benefices for 15 churches and chapels on an area of 140,000 acres : the percentage stood at 8·2 for a population of about 30,000.

In Bala there were only five churches and four clergymen for an area of 60,000 acres; the percentage stood at 7·3. In Dolgelley 11 benefices and 13 buildings for an area of 145,000 acres: the percentage stood at 8·9 for a population of 13,000. In Corwen clergy and churches had attained an equilibrium, there being 15 of each for an area of 124,000 acres: the percentage of attendance was 9·2 for a population of 15,400. There can be no question (one would think) as to the inadequacy of the Church's equipment both in men and buildings—in men more particularly, for no good can come of buildings without a proportionate supply of ministers, the only effect of disproportion being that no churches are adequately served, and that the population slips away to places where they can obtain more numerous opportunities of worshipping.

APPENDIX D.

Mr. Osborne Morgan's assertion that the Welsh have a natural antipathy to the doctrines and order of the Church of England is gainsayed by the fact that the Church is strong in many parts of Welsh Wales. We cite below, in illustration of this, some groups of contiguous parishes with agricultural populations in the most decidedly Welshy portions of St. David's Diocese. We might extend the list if it were necessary. The three groups cited lie apart from each other at considerable intervals, and we believe that the intermediate parishes would exhibit no very dissimilar result. These groups supply evidence that the parishes selected for the so-called censuses of the Liberationists would not (even if they had not been mis-represented) be fair samples of the several condition of the Church in the

country parishes generally. We again assert that the
variations in the condition of the Church are strongly
marked, and that what is true of one district is untrue of
another. But when Mr. Morgan draws the conclusion that
paucity of attendance is evidence that there is an innate
prejudice against the Church, might not the same argument
be extended to the Nonconformist bodies, which exhibit a
similar tendency to unequal distribution in various parts
of Wales. In the western counties of North Wales, for
instance, Baptists are comparatively few; in Pembrokeshire
they are very numerous. In the former districts Calvinistic
Methodism is greatly in the ascendant; in South Wales
Congregationalism holds that position. Might it not be
argued that there was something in the doctrines of the
Baptists which rendered them " alien " to the inhabitants
of Carnarvonshire, and something in the tenets of the Calvinistic Methodists " alien " to the Pembrokeshire people,
and, in short, something " alien " to the inhabitants of every
county of Wales in all the religious systems except the
one which happens to be predominant in that county ? The
geographical distribution of the Nonconformist bodies is
well worthy of observation, as showing that the predominance of any one body is due to other causes than an *à priori*
tendency of mind for a certain kind of doctrine or Church
polity. There is, at all events, no greater evidence of
" alienism " as regards the Church than as regards Nonconformity; and we believe this to be evidenced by the
condition of the Church in the following groups of parishes,
as shown in the proportion which the communicants bear
to the population :—

GROUP 1.—Six adjacent benefices on the mid-course of
the Tivy, viz. :—Llanfihangel-ar-Arth, Llandyssil, Llangeler,
Bangor with Henllan, Llanwenog, and Llanllwni with
Llanfihangel-Rhos-y-corn—1,216 communicants to a population of 9,213. or 13 per cent.

GROUP 2.—Six adjacent benefices on the course of the Towy between Carmarthen and Llandilo, viz.:—Abergwili, Llangunnor, Llanegwad, Llanarthney, Llangathen, and Llanfihangel-Aberbythick—894 communicants to a population of 7,489, or 12 per cent.

GROUP 3.—Six adjacent benefices in North Cardiganshire, viz.:—Llanrhystid, Llansantffraed, Llangwyryfon, Llauddeiniol, Llanychaiarn, and Llanilar with Rhostie —875 communicants to a population of 5,061, or 17 per cent.

One point of interest yet remains to be noticed. There exists a record of the number of communicants in Cardiganshire in 1804 as returned on the occasion of Bishop Burgess's primary visitation. This (be it observed) was before the secession of the Methodists from the Church in 1811. No diminution has occurred in the proportion which the number of communicants bears to the population in the present day as compared with 1804.

VACHER & SONS, Printers, 29, Parliament Street, and 62, Millbank Street.